INTO THE

ALEX MUR

<u>Content</u>

Dreamimagine.express

GET YOUR FREE BOOK

POETRYJOURNAL

PoetryJournal Dream.Imagine.express

Dedicated to the passion of writing and the love of poetry; writing for the love of poetry and its many interpretations, and I hope that the many readers that read this book find something that they can relate to and appreciate. A fiction writing that thrives on ideals relating to the appreciation of imagination utilisation, to dream, imagine and express.

Subscribe to website:

Kane's Wiki

Kane is a balanced individual, open-minded with a positive state of mind. In some instances, these are some of the qualities that the people around him relate with the most. For example, he is very respectful, treats everybody around him equally the same and is always willing to help. He is a forward thinker, most of all he is willing to stand and defend what he believes in. His mindset remained consistent with his outlook on life until things took a turn for the worse as he discovered his mother is suffering from cancer.

The story starts with the depiction of the beginning of the end when his mother died. His view on life became bleak. He suffered immensely mentally and emotionally. The one other potential anchor that existed for him, was his girlfriend Amani. Considering their relationship was developing and at the time not quite mature. In the end, she was the one person that almost soothes his pain, providing relief for him; making him further entertain the thought that there may be life after his mother's passing.His relationship with Amani continued to develop into something special, reopening his mind to possibilities of where he thought he may survive through his trauma.

ONE

Kane stared into the abyss. His mind was on constant rewind. He was emotional, and his anger was so apparent that it felt like it could metastasise and become tangible any minute. He attempted to console himself and calm down. He backed away from the edge for the first time in a while. Convenient, as he was almost at the point of imploding; a result of the continuous pressure he felt and the loss of loved ones which had now taken its toll on him. All he had in the world was himself so far as he was concerned. His mom — the descendant of a strong bloodline and the person who he considered to be his anchor — was the one he looked to in times like this. She was always willing and always took over and directed the situation, providing guidance along the way.

He would always ask her, "How do you do that?"

"Do what?" she always retorted, and then would chuckle. This exchange occurred like clockwork over the years, but not anymore.

He retreated from the side of the motorway, went back to his red BMW, and sped off into the wind hoping to empty his troubled mind of the one person who meant everything to him in this world — his mother.

Life would never be the same again. The distress continued, so he forced himself to forget about his situation.

He knocked on his girlfriend's door. She lived in East London, Homerton; a place he considered to be fairly okay. He resided in North London, Haringey, close to his mother, and he had loved the area because he loved being around her. Unfortunately, he no longer appreciated this living arrangement as his mother was no longer there.

"Hello, handsome" she said with a smile. She was trying to distract him; she could always tell when he was in a mood. Anticipating his response, she pulled him inside with vigour. They would usually play fight during their initial meetings, but not on this occasion. She brought him to the table where she had dinner waiting. A sudden euphoria, brought on by her kindness, built up inside as he was relieved from some of the stress he had been feeling. He showed his appreciation by kissing her again.

Amani smiled. She enjoyed looking after her man. Although Kane would not admit it, she had grown to be a significant part of his life. Apart from his mom, she was the only other person who could get through to him. She was also a strong woman. She was named after the queen of the Kush Empire, Amanirenas. Her father, Benjamin, had given her that name. Given that he was a militant individual and held his daughter in the highest esteem, the name was only fitting. He had always taught her to be strong, and to be proud of her heritage.

Amani's phone rang and shattered the mood between her and Kane.

"Hi Mom," she said as she breathed deeply, hinting to Kane that this would take a while. She left the room in the hope of restoring the tranquillity that Kane had garnered before her mom's abrupt interruption. However, Kane was grateful for the disruption; he drifted back into his mind and contemplated in silence.

Kane tried to tackle the immense sorrow of not only having lost his mom, but of now having to organise her burial as well. The first person who popped into his mind was his father, and almost immediately his face twisted. They had never had a good relationship, but he knew deep down that his father had loved his mother, Kelly-Ann. If there was one thing that Kane had in common with his father, it was that they were both equally stubborn. Still, they would have to remain civil on this occasion out of respect for his mother.

TWO

"My 'Jamaican Calypso' as I would always refer to her," Dane, Kane's father, said in a strong Jamaican accent."We grew up together as teenagers, and all through those years, I would tell her that she was going to be my baby mother one day." Everybody in the church laughed, including the pastor. As Dane began to get emotional, he wrapped things up and thanked everybody for coming to celebrate the life of his special girl, Mrs. Kelly-Ann Campbell — his dear wife.

Kane was not one for public speeches. He preferred to have his wounds tended to in seclusion. The thought of people taking pity on him was sickening. He stayed quiet and remained calm while his father openly mourned. He did not mind his father's vulgar speech, so long as he had remained respectful. Kane was currently short on patience, especially when it concerned his dear mother.

The Enfield Church held a great number of people; his mother was a kind soul, and she was loved by many in the community. Kane left the church accompanied by Amani. She drove them back to her place where she tried her best to cheer him up and distract him from his predicament. He genuinely appreciated her gesture even more because he cared for her deeply. They retired to bed for an early night while trying to console each other. Amani was hurting because she felt the pain that Kane was in. Kane became belligerent. He knew his true nature very well, so he decided to take a walk instead of picking a fight with the one person he knew he could lose too.

Kane got into his car. He decided to drive down the road to Hackney central to see his friend Julius, another Jamaican-born man who had a wild streak and loved to party. He figured it was the best place to find some distraction. Julius was high-spirited and had a good soul, but he attracted a lot of bad company. For some reason, Kane seemed to be the one who was always running into Julius's problems.

"Bredrin!" Julius shouted at a distance as he spotted Kane coming from afar. His voice reverberated through the street. Julius was a powerful man, dark-skinned and standing 6ft 2" tall, wearing dark sunglasses. He loved Kane like a brother. They had known each other from a young age, and he was one of Kane's oldest friends.

"Yes, my brother!" Kane cried out as he approached Julius. They were now in their element; it had been a while. Julius already knew the situation with Kane's mother but chose not to mention it. He knew Kane well enough to know that this was what he preferred. Julius and Kane stood in the middle of the road, disrupting and congesting the street. They walked slowly towards a club outside of Hackney central station, underneath the bridge, where Julius usually organized parties and gatherings on Saturday nights. It was December 13th. Julius was well aware of the love people had for his parties around this time of the year so close to Christmas, and as always, he intended to make the most of it.

On their way into the club, someone bumped into Julius and a sense of foreboding erupted within Kane. He grimaced, a reaction caused by the facial exchange between Julius and the person who seemed to be looking for an excuse to start something and ruin Julius's night. It put Kane in an even worse mood.

"Do we have a problem?" Julius enquired as he continued to get angry. The guy frowned, then spat in Julius's face without warning. Immediately, the club security interrupted. Unfortunately for the guy, the security was a friend of Julius's. He had witnessed the exchange and dragged the stranger away from Julius before throwing him into the road, causing cars to screech as everybody stopped to avoid hitting the stranger. It was quite a feat. Judging by the look of the security guard, to exercise such brute force was no problem. The security guard shouted to the stranger in the road, "Are you dumb, what were you thinking?"

The security guard then walked back to check on Julius.

Suddenly, the stranger recovered and pulled out a gun. He spared no bullets as he shot toward the club and then ran away into the night, leaving the security guard dead on the floor. Julius was fighting for his life in Kane's arms, only lasting a few minutes before he lost consciousness.

THREE

Kane was at the hospital visiting Julius. It had been a year since the unfortunate event that had resulted in Julius falling into a coma after suffering trauma to the head caused by the bullet. Every Friday, Kane would come and share his thoughts with Julius about current affairs, hoping that Julius would respond and make a joke. However, so far, all his efforts had been in vain."Kane." Doctor Bailey spoke after knocking on the door. He liked Kane so he made sure that his routine visits to check on Julius were while Kane was around. Kane always remained optimistic where his friend was concerned. Doctor Bailey made it his business to be consistent with Julius's care. Consequently, he had become committed to the care and well-being of Julius and his friend.

"Your Missus must be wondering where you are Kane. Maybe give her a call.""No need, Doc. She has been on the warpath today so I'm giving her some space until I've had a catch-up with young Jules," he said cheekily.

The doctor left the room to continue working as he was still on shift.

Kane decided to take a slow walk home from Homerton Hospital to Amani's house where they now lived together. Kane continued to dwell on the night of Julius's shooting. What was even more frustrating was that the police had neglected his friend's case, classifying the shooting as gang violence.

"How pathetic!" he regurgitated to himself repeatedly. Frustration compelled Kane to take matters into his own hands, but at this moment in time, even if he wanted to, he did not know where to start. Kane decided that he needed more time to clear his head. Consequently, he walked past his house, hearing the TV blaring as usual. Amani loved to watch horror movies on the weekend. He smiled as he thought about her habits and how he found them to be cute.

Kane walked to the end of the exceedingly long road that he now lived on and then continued to Kingsmead fields. There he stood and looked across the field in the dark. An unwavering feeling of loneliness washed over him, but he was too stubborn to admit or acknowledge its presence. He began to feel frustrated again, so he headed back to his house. On his journey, he encountered a stranger. He did not quite recognise him but there was something about him — Kane felt a familiar sense of foreboding that he had not experienced for a long time.

He walked past the stranger and noticed that there was a grimace and a smirk on his face. He was unaware of the reason for the stranger's attitude, and it made him uncomfortable. He decided to enquire. Kane quickly turned around and shouted.

"Don't I know you?"

The stranger, unbeknownst to Kane, suddenly ran towards him with his knife and stabbed him in his side as he retorted "You do!" in a Cockney accent.

Fortunately, Kane had always carried a gun since the night of the shooting. He managed to get one shot off before losing consciousness.

Kane woke up in Homerton Hospital. Amani was crying beside him, confused as to why her man was in this situation."Hey lover," Amani said in relief when his eyes opened. "You gave me quite a scare," she added, overwhelmed with emotion.

Kane did not respond. Instead, he jumped out of bed just as the police came in, forcing him to remain calm. The two white policemen introduced themselves.

"Good morning, mate. I am Detective Officer Rover and he is Officer Cole". Rover had a lean build with a bass tone to his voice and a compact build. The other, Cole, was built firmly with a Liverpool accent.

Rover appeared to be around 5ft 9" and carried himself like a leader. He was proud to show it. Kane guessed that he was the more experienced of the two.

They enquired about what had happened to him during the incident. He explained that he had had an altercation with a stranger who had run up to him and attacked him.

"We found two traces of blood at the scene, but we did not find any evidence of a weapon."

Kane had flashbacks the minute that the officer spoke. He started remembering the struggle after he had used the gun as well as the struggle that had followed, causing the gun to fall and slip away into a nearby river. That explained the missing gun. The stranger had run off once the situation had got out of hand.

Officer Cole continued to explain that they needed to piece everything together. "This is where you come in mate." He looked at Kane with an expectant expression. Kane wished that he could wipe it from his face, but all he cared about was that the painkillers were wearing off.

Kane began to tell his story. He made sure he was careful with his words. The less they knew, the better. He intended to sort out his problems on his own, and if he were to find the stranger again, he would take care of it, for Jules, once and for all.

The police officers left the hospital frustrated. They knew that Kane was lying but there was nothing they could prove. "Didn't record any evidence of the altercation, useless shit." Detective Cole exclaimed angrily to his partner on their way out of the hospital.

"You may be able to lie to them, that's a given, but don't try that with me, Kane..." Amani continued to press for information about what had happened to him. "It wouldn't make a difference if I said I got stung by a bee, would it?" Kane said with a smile.

Amani did not find any pleasure in his statement. She threw her handbag at Kane's wound. He reacted to catch it, but the movement caused his wound to start hurting him again, even with the extra codeine in his system. Kane gave in as he knew that she was just getting started. He explained the situation to her, and she reacted with anger that then turned into more worries, which was what he wanted to avoid.

Kane left the hospital a week later, assisted by Amani and his father. He could not wait to go back home. Dane drove them back in his blue Toyota Hybrid. Dane and Kane said the bare minimum to each other. Amani was astonished as she knew that they had never got on too well, but she had never witnessed it before.

As they approached their home, Kane felt another sense of foreboding wash over him. He asked his father to drive straight past the house instead. He did not feel that it was wise or safe to go home given his current situation and recent events. He ended up staying at his mom's house. Kane had not been there since she had died and the memories of her stirred within him for the first few hours. His father did not stay long. He helped Kane into the house and then gave him a look of acknowledgement before departing.

"Who knew you two had telepathy," Amani said sarcastically, rolling her eyes."Do not start please. I've had enough of your bullshit today," Kane retorted."You speak to me like that again and I'll show you more than telepathy," Amani replied in kind.

"I will do what I like so please stop," Kane said sternly.She knew when she had pushed him too far, so she paused and then left to go to the living room to cool off.

Amani prepared dinner in the evening as Kane rested to further recuperate. Conveniently for Kane, it gave him time to think. He had flashes of the events that had taken place earlier. He had decided not to stop at home for a couple of reasons; the suspicious vans that were parked too close to the house, and the fact that he thought he recognised one of the individuals walking past as the person who had stabbed him. There was something about his face and the feeling he had experienced for the second time now. Kane began to wonder whether they really were random attacks as they did not add up.

FOUR

Idi Isiah woke up in a pleasant mood. Today he was liberated from his shackles and his imprisonment at Her Majesty's Holloway Prison Correctional Facility, where he had spent the last 10 years of his life. For most people, a special occasion such as this would be a time of optimism and opportunity for a better life. For Idi, it was a time of torment, as he contemplated his revenge on the individuals that he held responsible as the very reason why he had remained behind bars the past decade. He contemplated his options and grew disgusted. He was hungry for revenge to the point that it consumed him. Being caught by the police on a gun and drug charge was not what he had planned for his future. Most of his family had disowned him shortly after, once the information that his gun was being connected to murders, and individuals were being hospitalised as a result of his actions, was released. They moved away, destroying the only community he knew, and cut off all contact with him.

He would never admit that the actions that caused his imprisonment were his fault, that he had been caught with drugs in his possession, or that the situation leading to him being captured by police was by chance. He wanted revenge for his girl Caron who had been murdered, someone who was close to his heart and incredibly special. Her murder had caused his incarceration in Idi's mind, as it had provoked the police to attempt to find him which had led to the gun and drugs discovery.

Despite his thoughts of revenge, he smiled knowing that by the end of the day, he would have had accomplished his goal and wiped his enemies from existence — should everything go as planned. He did not have money but the people he had connections to would be happy to help him, given the fact that he had not given them up during his incarceration. Despite his dark affliction, he was loyal to his commitments. This not only made him useful in his line of business but dangerous at the same time.

On December 13th, Idi was released from prison at noon. He wandered down the road with nothing but a £50 note in his pocket, "Get a gun," He thought to himself. His first stop was Wood Green, where he went to see one of his long-time employers, Marlon Dean.

"My Lord [Jamaican accent]". He greeted him with a hug that felt like a cold embrace, he only knew the guy as a killer.

"You just got out today mate, what brings you here? Shouldn't you be laying low?" Marlon said calmly. "I don't want you jeopardising my place of business so unfortunately, I have nothing to offer you," he added, speaking slowly with a smile.

"I want some tools, mate. You owe me that much," Idi retorted after about a minute of silence."I don't owe you shit," Marlon said explosively."Based on our history of loyalty in business, why not?" he asked calmly, after going from one hundred to zero with his emotions.

They concluded their conversation after Idi negotiated his demands.

On August 29th in the summer of 2009 (ten years ago), Julius woke up around six in the morning. He needed time to acclimate and prepare for the long day ahead. He prepared himself some strong coffee for breakfast. He then freshened up, got his gun, and then left his flat in Forest

Gate. He was dressed in a grey Adidas tracksuit with orange stripes that ran down the sides and trainers. Caron Parker worked on Wood Street. He waited diligently until 5 in the afternoon for when she would leave her office to go home.

She was a voluptuous and beautiful dark-skinned woman who knew how to dress and carry herself in a womanly fashion, especially on workdays. She was always promptly on time for work, and she was the first one to leave. He approached her as she made her way to the bus stop to go home. She knew who he was but was puzzled as to why he was watching her.

"C'mon Julius, please." she pleaded for him to believe her."You know what am looking for and you know you can't leave until I have it."

She trembled beneath his knees as he pointed the gun at her. He had no intention of using it, but she did not know that. She was alarmed and feared for her life.

The motorway was busy as they made their way directly under the bridge of the motorway, overseeing the train tracks in Leytonstone. Julius began to lose patience so he upped the stakes. He pulled the trigger back and extended his arm with the gun.

"Idi's stash. I know you know where it is. You two have that Bonnie and Clyde thing going on, so I'll ask you once more: Where?" He shouted, with so much emphasis that he forgot to keep the gun in check. Julius shot Caron directly in the head, killing her instantly. He ran to his car and sped off, his heart racing. He had killed before, but he had never killed a woman, or anyone by mistake like this.

Sonny kept talking. As usual, his mouth was restless, and Idi did not want to hear him speak anymore. He was eager to get this business exchange over and done with. He just wanted to collect the money in exchange for the drugs in the boot so then he could disappear and not hear Sonny utter another word. Sonny was the driver while Julius was running an errand for Marlon. Things were going well as he started the day by having sex with his main girl, Caron. It always put him in a positive mood and gave him a personal high that always gave him comfort as he worked through the day.

A police car approached them in Stratford. He was puzzled, but routine and protocols convinced him to forget his thoughts and stay calm. Unfortunately, Sonny had had some cocaine that morning which left him in an even worse mood, especially in the sight of the approaching officer.

"Idi Isiah, could you come out of the car please?" The officer asked, speaking through a loudspeaker.

He complied and they retreated closer to the officer's car as they spoke. Sonny continued to sweat, given the unpredictability of the situation.

"Don't worry, this stop has nothing to do with you. However, we have some bad news about your girlfriend. We decided to get in touch because you conveniently drove past, and you are listed as her contact in case of emergencies."

"C'mon, officer, let us hear it," Idi replied after the officer's long introduction to their conversation.

"Caron has been involved in a homicide," he said calmly. "I will let you go but should you think of any information, here is my card. Please let me know."

He walked him back to the car only to notice Sonny's demeanour. He had been sweating and had a stench of paranoia about him.

The officer became suspicious. He decided to search the car and discovered a key of cocaine, a pistol, and a sawn-off shotgun.

FIVE

December 20th, 2019 (present-day)

"A blast from the fucking past!" Kane said in a loud and vulgar tone.

"What did you say, honey?" Amani replied in reaction to his outburst, thinking that Kane was talking to her from afar.

"Sorry hun, Arsenal is losing, that's all," he replied in a jovial tone.

He resumed his wonderment. He had thought long and hard about his enemies and concluded that he had a small handful.He then thought about Julius's enemies and could hardly keep them to ten fingers.However, there was a situation that stood out that had his mind screaming for revenge.

He recalled one particular time that Julius had spoken about, a moment that had changed him and his life trajectory, as it had haunted him every day since it had taken place. In his mind, Julius was a crooked criminal but a criminal with a code. He felt remorse after killing Caron as he saw her as innocent. What made things more complicated is that he had killed the lover of someone he did business with, and they had the same boss.

Marlon knew that Julius was not to be trusted, and he had him followed and watched constantly. He never trusted him, but Julius was a good worker and highly effective, hence the reason he kept him on his payroll. However, considering Julius' recent growth of conscience after killing Caron, he decided that he was of no use to him, subsequently making it known to Idi that Julius was the one that had killed his girl 10 years ago. Unfortunately, Idi had been brought up on charges before he could act on his revenge — until now. Julius knew that Idi was a problem but after his incarceration, he had never seen him as a threat until it was too late. Kane did not want to make that mistake.

Idi was sloppy. He knew he was still alive by luck. He had been shot on the outside of his shoulder but fortunately for him, it was a flesh wound. He made his escape to an abandoned building in Victoria Park where they found an old club gym. There he found some old clothes to pressure the wound until the blood began to clot. He made his way back home where he sewed up his skin to close the wound, and then used some dressing from a first aid box he had found in the gym.

"I need your help and based on our history, you owe me big time, so do this for me and we are even. Otherwise, I will kill you and that is a promise, Sonny!"

Sonny had been out of prison five years before, but he knew Idi would come knocking one day. Therefore, he kept his mouth shut and did as commanded because he was scared. Idi knew that if he pressed him hard enough, Sonny would fold instantly, being the coward that he was. That was their secret, but everybody gave him the time of day because of his boss, Marlon. Idi didn't care and Sonny knew it.

"Sure, of course. Whatever you need," he pleaded with Idi, who was fuming.

"Oh yeah and Sonny? We need manpower," Idi said with a grimace.

Idi got Sonny's contact number from Marlon and within minutes of speaking with Sonny, he found out where Kane lived. On the day of Kane's release from the hospital, he stayed waiting outside his house, counting on the fact that Kane didn't know what he looked like. However, he did not know that Kane knew about Sonny through Julius and that Sonny's reputation of being a coward preceded him. Sonny was a coward, but he had a lot of bona fide gangsters and killers around him. He could be particularly useful which was the only reason Idi kept him alive.

"He'll live, for now," he admitted to himself, knowing he was just itching to blow Sonny away. He still blamed him for getting arrested. Sonny did not have him locked up, but he did inform Idi. He saw that as the logic for Sonny only receiving a five-year sentence, whereas he had had ten whole years taken from his life.

Sonny knew too much, and he was too weak to keep his big mouth shut. Cold and calculating, like a chessboard, Idi devised his plans several steps in advance.

SIX

Wednesday, December 25th, 2019. Christmas day was positive. Despite the onset of the prevailing issues that had followed him the past few weeks, he was determined to forget his issues and allowed himself to enjoy the day, if only for the sake of Amani. Amani took the day off. She was not a true believer in the Bible, but she respected the whole idea of Christmas being family-oriented. For the past five years, she had taken the night off to spend the day with her man. She arrived home feeling great and looking great — she was a beautiful soul in and out. Kane was mesmerised and continued to watch her as she arrived outside his mother's house and exited the car. She spoke aloud to her father on the phone about her mother, while entering the front door. It showed that she came from a close and well-knit family.

However, that was not what was on Kane's mind. Ever since he had taken over his mother's business a year ago. It was a residential care business that she had run for the greater part of her mature years coming up to 25 years total, she had decided that she wanted to retire and lead a different life. As always, he liberated her and encouraged her to look after herself and put her health before anything. But it was around this time that she had been diagnosed with an advanced stage of cancer and told that she had little time left to live. Impressively, she died five years after, which was a true testament to her strength and

21

character. She fought all the way. It was not pretty but it was her way and all she knew.

Conveniently, as Amani entered the door, her conversation ended, when she saw Kane. The atmosphere changed between them, and he seductively approached her. She read between the lines and knew what he had in mind. They played their intimate game of resistance, mostly on her part, but eventually, she welcomed him in. They teased, licked, and tasted each other. He undressed her, caressing, and rediscovering all he classed as special about her, which was everything. She waited eagerly as he teased her, and he waited just enough until she erupted. His penetration was immense, and she sensed it all over her body as he played inside her and she screamed with desire for more. She climaxed for the second time as they continued to change and interchange, savouring every moment of their special time.

Her beautiful body was tight and there was a solid and tense connection between her legs as he lifted her up and back inside, opening her wider and wider as she motivated him to put all of himself inside her until they both broke down and gave into a synchronised moan and climaxed together. They kissed for a minute before falling asleep without changing position.

Kane woke up to a reign of destruction as bullets exploded from outside and into the house. He instantly covered Amani as he urgently gathered himself and pulled down her to the floor, waiting for whoever was shooting to stop. They continued their assault on Kane's mother's house for a minute before disappearing into a black sprinter van. Kane urgently began to assess Amani, trying to check if she was hurt. Amani had been hit in the arm by one of the bullets. Kane was fuming in anger with himself at the thought that he had risked her life by bringing danger her way. The bullet appeared to have damaged her artery as she was bleeding profusely.

He did not hesitate, and he rushed her to the hospital, which took them about 15 minutes. When they arrived, Amani was losing consciousness, so he shouted for a doctor until he got someone's attention. He did not know how he would have continued living if anything had happened to her. He closed his eyes as tears built up as he tried to bear the contempt, remorse, and anger that he felt inside in a simultaneous eruption.

On Thursday at 6 am. Amani woke up and regained consciousness. She smiled as she caressed Kane's face. Kane did not wait for approval or resistance. He took Amani and disappeared from the hospital before anybody even noticed they were missing. He took her to her dad Benjamin's house. Her mom Elle-Ameen started to cry as soon as she saw her daughter, but the anger was apparent. Benjamin was full of it but composed nonetheless. Elle-Ameen and Benjamin helped her inside, and Kane thought that they had entered a haven, so he tried to calm down. Kane was in shock. He tried to speak and even forced himself but every time he attempted to utter a word, he began to break down at the sight of what had become of the love of his life.

Elle-Ameen's past years of nursing had come in handy. She was always prepared as a result of the years of her husband's warring escapades, due to him being from a criminal background. She attended to her daughter's de-stabilizing condition, as her pulse was becoming weaker. Elle-Ameen understood the situation and how to make her better; she was automatic in her response, and everything happened like clockwork when it came to handling Amani's condition. Kane and his father-in-law had issues coping. They remained shocked at the thought that it was someone so close to them having such complications in their life, at the onset of her appearing to develop further health problems. But hey were reminded how strong she was by her pulling through. This was one of the reasons why Kane had admired both mother and daughter, and mutually, her father shared the same feelings. Elle-Ameen made Amani stable again, she went back to sleep, and they watched over her for the first hour. They were all so focused on her that it appeared that time itself even stood still.

SEVEN

Kane stared down the barrel of the pistol aimed at his head. Alarm bells were ringing, a prime indication of him appreciating the magnitude of the situation.

"You promised me that my girl would always be safe, and you lied. Give me one reason I shouldn't kill you right here and right now?" Benjamin spoke calmly but he was stern.

"I will kill the people responsible for this. I'll accept whatever you think is best after I am done." Benjamin's body language indicated that this was not his first time pointing his gun with intent, so Kane knew that he had to speak with caution as one wrong word may have him killed. His family was what Benjamin lived for, and what he would die for should the situation call for that precise act.

Benjamin was serious and rightfully so, for his daughter was in bad shape and he held only one person accountable.

Kane was surprised at his level of composure in front of the gun, but he now realised that he would never be the same again. Ever since his mother had passed away, it was almost like losing a part of himself. It numbed him to the point that he welcomed death, except when he was with the only other person that he truly cared for, who was now in critical condition. He intended to make it right.

Kane did not love to fight but he knew how to. His father, Dane, had made sure of that. He had been a boxer since the age of 10 years old up to his 18th birthday when he quit. He was a true talent, but he did not want to pursue it. Kane and Dane's relationship had fractured because of his actions; his father saw everything as disrespect to him.

Kane and Benjamin figured out their issues and the hostility began to lift from the room. The door was shut and they were isolated, as this was a debate between two men that warranted no interruptions. Benjamin spoke anonymously[ominously]; he was organising an attempt to prepare to rectify the situation in reaction to his daughter and her current condition. As he intended to retaliate, he felt obligated to make sure that his family could never be hurt again by those responsible. He was deep in thought. It was clear that this was not his first situation where he had the intention of engaging in serious violence, and he knew the people who would help him to carry out his actions, judging by his conversations on the phone.

Within an hour, a black sprinter van parked outside the house, and Kane wondered who Benjamin really was. They made their way outside the house and greeted the men. Kane was on guard as Benjamin instructed him to enter the black van. Four black men with machetes and shotguns appeared as the van doors opened. The machetes had dried blood on them.

Four Rastafarians. Kane knew they were killers. He had seen that look before. Their intent was beyond apparent, but he didn't know whether to welcome their ride-along or to prepare for his demise. Either way, he was destined to find out. There was nothing distinctive about them. They were tall but slim, slender but strong, and even their clothes were low-grade to the point that they could be mistaken for homeless people. However, one thing that they could not change was the look in their eyes. He knew what killers looked like.

They rode quietly in the back of the van — everybody had bad intentions on their mind. They all knew that this day could be their last. Benjamin and Kane decided to look in the last place they expected to find their enemy, surmising that the best place to start their search was Sonny's house. Once again, Kane was at an advantage because of Julius and for that he was grateful. Julius knew Sonny's whereabouts due to him being affiliated with the same criminal organisation years back. He was counting on Sonny's lack of ability to be tactical and smart about his movements making him predictable to find. They made their way to locate him. However, he knew that Idi was not that stupid, and would not make it easy.

They drove past Sonny's house. They had been watching his house for over 12 hours without a whiff or hint of his presence. Eventually, Kane and Benjamin broke in. They didn't know where he could be, but this was no surprise as they knew how to stay low. An hour later, they wrapped things up and decided to take a drive back to Kane and Amani's house, have something to eat, and regroup.

When they arrived, driving towards the house, nostalgia kicked in. Kane decided to view his home from afar on the approach, and he experienced flashbacks and euphoric moments of when his woman was well, a long time before the current problems had started. His thoughts were suddenly interrupted by another nagging feeling as he noticed a car that he had seen before. He could not quite remember or place his suspicions until he saw Sonny aiming a shotgun through the car window. Benjamin began evasive manoeuvres as he approached Sonny in the car with the gun. At this point, there was no going back as Benjamin had already decided to commit even if it meant his death.

Sonny randomly shot at the car in a panic as the big van approached. Benjamin's intentions were to destroy both cars in the collision. Both parties began shooting and the bullets started ricocheting, causing casualties. Benjamin was shot, two of the dreads in the back died on collision and the others were injured. It was an execution that took three lives, and both cars were also destroyed, with Sonny inside dead on impact. Idi stood, stunned by the lengths that they had gone to. He had planned it perfectly, tracking Kane for hours ever since they had infiltrated Sonny's house. It was only by chance that he had driven away in his car and saw their approaching black van. Kane and Benjamin watched from afar and waited for their opportunity.

"That useless shit," Idi cursed about Sonny as he spat on the floor and ran to his car across the road, knowing the convenience of his death for he planned to kill him either way. He never anticipated that this would be the result but he murmured what he had concluded, "Only Sonny could fuck up a good plan."

Kane was shooting his semi-automatic. It ripped through the street to the point that Idi turned around and ran to the house. Idi kicked the door in and disappeared, and Kane pursued him.

Kane entered the house apprehensively. He knew Idi was waiting to ambush him on his entry into the house but he could not stop himself; he wanted it to end today once and for all, irrespective of the cost. He needed to make amends. He was aware that Idi had dropped his gun on the way in, so he knew he had the advantage.

Idi felt vulnerable without his gun to defend him, but he decided that being shot was not an option. He waited behind the door and surmised that it was not the best plan. He felt that it was the least expected action for him to take, and he had nothing to lose.

Idi grabbed Kane's hands from behind the door as he pointed his gun out upon his entry into his home. He managed to fire one shot that ricocheted off the steel table and into the window that had been recently replaced. Idi managed to subdue Kane and pushed the gun away from them as they struggled, knowing that he had his knife on him. He intended to use it and put Kane down once and for all. Kane anticipated as much.

Idi pulled his knife out in a slashing fashion to try and cut Kane. He was not successful. Kane anticipated this. He grabbed Idi's hand, the one that was holding the knife, and turned it. He now had him in a bear hug as he brutally pulled the knife toward him and Idi's chest. They

28

struggled for what seemed like a lifetime for Benjamin, but he waited because he felt Kane needed to handle the issue on his own. In his mind, this was a test to show that he could do what needed to be done.

The immense screaming from within the house as they fought came to an abrupt halt. It suddenly got quiet before there was a sharp pulling open of the door; Kane emerged. Cut and bruised, he looked shocked at what had just taken place, for he had taken Idi's life.

He knew that things could have gone either way between them as they fought, and despite the many fights he had been in, this had been the first time that he had ever taken a life.

Benjamin instinctively shook his head in approval.

EIGHT

December 25th, 2025

Kane helped Amani out of the car. She struggled as she tugged and pulled to get herself out of the car, then she worked hard to find her footing to balance her stance. She felt amazement at how things had changed, especially since they had come so close to death over the years. She was grateful that the only issue she was bothered with now was the change involving her body, bearing in mind that she was seven months pregnant and was expecting sooner rather than later. In her mind, it was "scaring the shit out of her" as she had reiterated over the past few months. However, she remained grateful since Kane and her family had been there as she recovered from her life-threatening situation. Kane and Benjamin had become closer over the years, bonding over wanting to protect Amani.

Life for Kane and Benjamin had been peaceful, and they remained grateful but on guard, unwilling to retire as pandemonium seemed to occur when it was least expected.

They made their way to a celebratory meal with Amani's parents, a tradition that they now consistently practiced every Sunday. Fittingly, on this occasion, it was also Christmas Day, which they considered to be a time of family appreciation.

They were slow in their preparations to leave home but that had become common recently, Amani complained as she struggled to find decent-sized clothing to wear due to her predicament; she blamed Kane and cursed the day she met him. Kane did not take notice. He knew that she was constantly trying to push his buttons and he was in too good of a mood to play her games. Plus, he was contemplating the journey that he had taken over the last few years and he was feeling grateful for his accomplishments and the life he now got to see as the calm before the storm. However, if anybody were to ask what storm? He would retort, "Fuck knows."

Kane and Amani arrived to hear the drama between Benjamin and their mother as they argued over trivial issues, about something in the past that had happened to them in the 90s.

"Hello there, Mrs-." Kane was interrupted.

"I told you to stop with this 'Mrs.' a long time ago, Kane. You have been part of this family for far too long. I'm putting my foot down," Elle-Ameen complained.

He had always respected Amani's mother and loved her dearly. He always saw her like a queen, and she carried herself as such, so he always referred to her by her title — until now.

"Apologies, Mrs. Elle-Ameen," he joked.

"Hardhead, but you're getting there," she retorted.

It was a merry day indeed, and it showed how tight and close-knit the family had become over the years. Benjamin and Elle-Ameen knew that Kane did not have much time for his father and so they appreciated him being so respectful to them and their daughter. Because of this, they always treated him as family and appreciated the care he showed. They perceived it to be a special relationship.

Kane excused himself as he retreated to the bathroom. He admitted that he was aware that the relationship between him and his father was not the greatest and never would be, but he still felt responsible for checking in and showing his respects when the occasion demanded, knowing that his father appreciated it.

"Howdy," Kane said into the voicemail but before he could continue, his dad answered.

"Everything good?" Dane replied in a surprisingly pleasant tone.

"Everything is good. Just showing my respects and making sure you're still in one piece" Kane expressed.

"A lot of people have been doing that around you recently, have you ended up not being alright?" He was referring to Kane's now past years of violence.

Kane went quiet, having felt the urge to cut the conversation short.

"Thanks for looking out for me Dane. I am glad you care," Kane said sarcastically.

"Right, I mean, I am your dad, after all," Dane pleaded in a not so calm tone.

"Are you?" Kane retorted before hanging up abruptly.

He admitted that his dad knew how to push his buttons with his righteous, judgmental... He stopped his thoughts, calmed himself, hung up, and returned to the living room.

Amani welcomed him with open arms and a kiss. Her parents had already retired to their bedroom for the night.

As usual, Amani could read her man like a book, and she could sense the annoyance from the look on his face. She knew that Kane usually checked in with his father on days such as these; usually with a smile on his face as he would leave the best until last, which would be his final call to his mother. This was because his dad would usually leave him feeling frustrated, then his mom would calm him down. On this occasion, Amani felt that it was her responsibility to keep him balanced and positive on a day that they both devoted to being family-oriented.

Amani and Kane prepared for their departure from Amani's parent's house. They suddenly felt the need to be alone in their domain, so they were brief with their goodbyes before getting into Kane's car. It was night and it was approaching 11:30 pm. They quietly departed. Their mood was pleasant yet tranquil; thus, they made their way home.

NINE

Kane stared into the abyss. His mind was on constant rewind. He was emotional, and his anger was so apparent that it felt like it could metastasise and become tangible any minute. He attempted to console himself and calm down. He backed away from the edge for the first time in a while. Convenient, as he was almost at the point of imploding; a result of the continuous pressure he felt and the loss of loved ones which had now taken its toll on him. All he had in the world was himself so far as he was concerned. His mom — the descendant of a strong bloodline and the person who he considered to be his anchor — was the one he looked to in times like this. She was always willing and always took over and directed the situation, providing guidance along the way.

He would always ask her, "How do you do that?"

"Do what?" she always retorted, and then would chuckle. This exchange occurred like clockwork over the years, but not anymore.

He retreated from the side of the motorway, went back to his red BMW, and sped off into the wind hoping to empty his troubled mind of the one person who meant everything to him in this world — his mother.

Life would never be the same again. The distress continued, so he forced himself to forget about his situation.

He knocked on his girlfriend's door. She lived in East London, Homerton; a place he considered to be fairly okay. He resided in North London, Haringey, close to his mother, and he had loved the area because he loved being around her. Unfortunately, he no longer appreciated this living arrangement as his mother was no longer there.

"Hello, handsome" she said with a smile. She was trying to distract him; she could always tell when he was in a mood. Anticipating his response, she pulled him inside with vigour. They would usually play fight during their initial meetings, but not on this occasion. She brought him to the table where she had dinner waiting. A sudden euphoria, brought on by her kindness, built up inside as he was relieved from some of the stress he had been feeling. He showed his appreciation by kissing her again.

Amani smiled. She enjoyed looking after her man. Although Kane would not admit it, she had grown to be a significant part of his life. Apart from his mom, she was the only other person who could get through to him. She was also a strong woman. She was named after the queen of the Kush Empire, Amanirenas. Her father, Benjamin, had given her that name. Given that he was a militant individual and held his daughter in the highest esteem, the name was only fitting. He had always taught her to be strong, and to be proud of her heritage.

Amani's phone rang and shattered the mood between her and Kane.

"Hi Mom," she said as she breathed deeply, hinting to Kane that this would take a while. She left the room in the hope of restoring the tranquillity that Kane had garnered before her mom's abrupt interruption. However, Kane was grateful for the disruption; he drifted back into his mind and contemplated in silence.

Kane tried to tackle the immense sorrow of not only having lost his mom, but of now having to organise her burial as well. The first person who popped into his mind was his father, and almost immediately his face twisted. They had never had a good relationship, but he knew deep down that his father had loved his mother, Kelly-Ann. If there was one thing that Kane had in common with his father, it was that they were both equally stubborn. Still, they would have to remain civil on this occasion out of respect for his mother.

TEN

"My 'Jamaican Calypso' as I would always refer to her," Dane, Kane's father, said in a strong Jamaican accent. "We grew up together as teenagers, and all through those years, I would tell her that she was going to be my baby mother one day." Everybody in the church laughed, including the pastor. As Dane began to get emotional, he wrapped things up and thanked everybody for coming to celebrate the life of his special girl, Mrs. Kelly-Ann Campbell — his dear wife.

Kane was not one for public speeches. He preferred to have his wounds tended to in seclusion. The thought of people taking pity on him was sickening. He stayed quiet and remained calm while his father openly mourned. He did not mind his father's vulgar speech, so long as he had remained respectful. Kane was currently short on patience, especially when it concerned his dear mother.

The Enfield Church held a great number of people; his mother was a kind soul, and she was loved by many in the community. Kane left the church accompanied by Amani. She drove them back to her place where she tried her best to cheer him up and distract him from his predicament. He genuinely appreciated her gesture even more because he cared for her deeply. They retired to bed for an early night while trying to console each other. Amani was hurting because she felt the pain that Kane was in. Kane became belligerent. He knew his true nature very well, so he decided to take a walk instead of picking a fight with the one person he knew he could lose too.

Kane got into his car. He decided to drive down the road to Hackney central to see his friend Julius, another Jamaican-born man who had a wild streak and loved to party. He figured it was the best place to find some distraction. Julius was high-spirited and had a good soul, but he attracted a lot of bad company. For some reason, Kane seemed to be the one who was always running into Julius's problems.

"Bredrin!" Julius shouted at a distance as he spotted Kane coming from afar. His voice reverberated through the street. Julius was a powerful man, dark-skinned and standing 6ft 2" tall, wearing dark sunglasses. He loved Kane like a brother. They had known each other from a young age, and he was one of Kane's oldest friends.

"Yes, my brother!" Kane cried out as he approached Julius. They were now in their element; it had been a while. Julius already knew the situation with Kane's mother but chose not to mention it. He knew Kane well enough to know that this was what he preferred. Julius and Kane stood in the middle of the road, disrupting and congesting the street. They walked slowly towards a club outside of Hackney central station, underneath the bridge, where Julius usually organized parties and gatherings on Saturday nights. It was December 13th. Julius was well aware of the love people had for his parties around this time of the year so close to Christmas, and as always, he intended to make the most of it.

On their way into the club, someone bumped into Julius and a sense of foreboding erupted within Kane. He grimaced, a reaction caused by the facial exchange between Julius and the person who seemed to be looking for an excuse to start something and ruin Julius's night. It put Kane in an even worse mood.

"Do we have a problem?" Julius enquired as he continued to get angry.The guy frowned, then spat in Julius's face without warning.Immediately, the club security interrupted. Unfortunately for the guy, the security was a friend of Julius's. He had witnessed the exchange and dragged the stranger away from Julius before throwing him into the road, causing cars to screech as everybody stopped to avoid hitting the stranger. It was quite a feat. Judging by the look of the security guard, to exercise such brute force was no problem. The security guard shouted to the stranger in the road, "Are you dumb, what were you thinking?"

The security guard then walked back to check on Julius.

Suddenly, the stranger recovered and pulled out a gun. He spared no bullets as he shot toward the club and then ran away into the night, leaving the security guard dead on the floor. Julius was fighting for his life in Kane's arms, only lasting a few minutes before he lost consciousness.

ELEVEN

Kane was at the hospital visiting Julius. It had been a year since the unfortunate event that had resulted in Julius falling into a coma after suffering trauma to the head caused by the bullet. Every Friday, Kane would come and share his thoughts with Julius about current affairs, hoping that Julius would respond and make a joke. However, so far, all his efforts had been in vain."Kane." Doctor Bailey spoke after knocking on the door. He liked Kane so he made sure that his routine visits to check on Julius were while Kane was around. Kane always remained optimistic where his friend was concerned. Doctor Bailey made it his business to be consistent with Julius's care. Consequently, he had become committed to the care and well-being of Julius and his friend.

"Your Missus must be wondering where you are Kane. Maybe give her a call.""No need, Doc. She has been on the warpath today so I'm giving her some space until I've had a catch-up with young Jules," he said cheekily.

The doctor left the room to continue working as he was still on shift.

Kane decided to take a slow walk home from Homerton Hospital to Amani's house where they now lived together. Kane continued to dwell on the night of Julius's shooting. What was even more frustrating was that the police had neglected his friend's case, classifying the shooting as gang violence.

"How pathetic!" he regurgitated to himself repeatedly. Frustration compelled Kane to take matters into his own hands, but at this moment in time, even if he wanted to, he did not know where to start. Kane decided that he needed more time to clear his head. Consequently, he walked past his house, hearing the TV blaring as usual. Amani loved to watch horror movies on the weekend. He smiled as he thought about her habits and how he found them to be cute.

Kane walked to the end of the exceedingly long road that he now lived on and then continued to Kingsmead fields. There he stood and looked across the field in the dark. An unwavering feeling of loneliness washed over him, but he was too stubborn to admit or acknowledge its presence. He began to feel frustrated again, so he headed back to his house. On his journey, he encountered a stranger. He did not quite recognise him but there was something about him — Kane felt a familiar sense of foreboding that he had not experienced for a long time.

He walked past the stranger and noticed that there was a grimace and a smirk on his face. He was unaware of the reason for the stranger's attitude, and it made him uncomfortable. He decided to enquire. Kane quickly turned around and shouted.

"Don't I know you?"

The stranger, unbeknownst to Kane, suddenly ran towards him with his knife and stabbed him in his side as he retorted "You do!" in a Cockney accent.

Fortunately, Kane had always carried a gun since the night of the shooting. He managed to get one shot off before losing consciousness.

Kane woke up in Homerton Hospital. Amani was crying beside him, confused as to why her man was in this situation. "Hey lover," Amani said in relief when his eyes opened. "You gave me quite a scare," she added, overwhelmed with emotion.

Kane did not respond. Instead, he jumped out of bed just as the police came in, forcing him to remain calm. The two white policemen introduced themselves.

"Good morning, mate. I am Detective Officer Rover and he is Officer Cole". Rover had a lean build with a bass tone to his voice and a compact build. The other, Cole, was built firmly with a Liverpool accent.

Rover appeared to be around 5ft 9" and carried himself like a leader. He was proud to show it. Kane guessed that he was the more experienced of the two.

They enquired about what had happened to him during the incident. He explained that he had had an altercation with a stranger who had run up to him and attacked him.

"We found two traces of blood at the scene, but we did not find any evidence of a weapon."

Kane had flashbacks the minute that the officer spoke. He started remembering the struggle after he had used the gun as well as the struggle that had followed, causing the gun to fall and slip away into a nearby river. That explained the missing gun. The stranger had run off once the situation had got out of hand.

Officer Cole continued to explain that they needed to piece everything together. "This is where you come in mate." He looked at Kane with an expectant expression. Kane wished that he could wipe it from his face, but all he cared about was that the painkillers were wearing off.

Kane began to tell his story. He made sure he was careful with his words. The less they knew, the better. He intended to sort out his problems on his own, and if he were to find the stranger again, he would take care of it, for Jules, once and for all.

The police officers left the hospital frustrated. They knew that Kane was lying but there was nothing they could prove. "Didn't record any evidence of the altercation, useless shit." Detective Cole exclaimed angrily to his partner on their way out of the hospital.

"You may be able to lie to them, that's a given, but don't try that with me, Kane..." Amani continued to press for information about what had happened to him. "It wouldn't make a difference if I said I got stung by a bee, would it?" Kane said with a smile.

Amani did not find any pleasure in his statement. She threw her handbag at Kane's wound. He reacted to catch it, but the movement caused his wound to start hurting him again, even with the extra codeine in his system. Kane gave in as he knew that she was just getting started. He explained the situation to her, and she reacted with anger that then turned into more worries, which was what he wanted to avoid.

Kane left the hospital a week later, assisted by Amani and his father. He could not wait to go back home. Dane drove them back in his blue Toyota Hybrid. Dane and Kane said the bare minimum to each other. Amani was astonished as she knew that they had never got on too well, but she had never witnessed it before.

As they approached their home, Kane felt another sense of foreboding wash over him. He asked his father to drive straight past the house instead. He did not feel that it was wise or safe to go home given his current situation and recent events. He ended up staying at his mom's house. Kane had not been there since she had died and the memories of her stirred within him for the first few hours. His father did not stay long. He helped Kane into the house and then gave him a look of acknowledgement before departing.

"Who knew you two had telepathy," Amani said sarcastically, rolling her eyes."Do not start please. I've had enough of your bullshit today," Kane retorted."You speak to me like that again and I'll show you more than telepathy," Amani replied in kind.

"I will do what I like so please stop," Kane said sternly.She knew when she had pushed him too far, so she paused and then left to go to the living room to cool off.

Amani prepared dinner in the evening as Kane rested to further recuperate. Conveniently for Kane, it gave him time to think. He had flashes of the events that had taken place earlier. He had decided not to stop at home for a couple of reasons; the suspicious vans that were parked too close to the house, and the fact that he thought he recognised one of the individuals walking past as the person who had stabbed him. There was something about his face and the feeling he had experienced for the second time now. Kane began to wonder whether they really were random attacks as they did not add up.

TWELVE

Idi Isiah woke up in a pleasant mood. Today he was liberated from his shackles and his imprisonment at Her Majesty's Holloway Prison Correctional Facility, where he had spent the last 10 years of his life. For most people, a special occasion such as this would be a time of optimism and opportunity for a better life. For Idi, it was a time of torment, as he contemplated his revenge on the individuals that he held responsible as the very reason why he had remained behind bars the past decade. He contemplated his options and grew disgusted. He was hungry for revenge to the point that it consumed him. Being caught by the police on a gun and drug charge was not what he had planned for his future. Most of his family had disowned him shortly after, once the information that his gun was being connected to murders, and individuals were being hospitalised as a result of his actions, was released. They moved away, destroying the only community he knew, and cut off all contact with him.

He would never admit that the actions that caused his imprisonment were his fault, that he had been caught with drugs in his possession, or that the situation leading to him being captured by police was by chance. He wanted revenge for his girl Caron who had been murdered, someone who was close to his heart and incredibly special. Her murder had caused his incarceration in Idi's mind, as it had provoked the police to attempt to find him which had led to the gun and drugs discovery.

Despite his thoughts of revenge, he smiled knowing that by the end of the day, he would have had accomplished his goal and wiped his enemies from existence — should everything go as planned. He did not have money but the people he had connections to would be happy to help him, given the fact that he had not given them up during his incarceration. Despite his dark affliction, he was loyal to his commitments. This not only made him useful in his line of business but dangerous at the same time.

On December 13th, Idi was released from prison at noon. He wandered down the road with nothing but a £50 note in his pocket, "Get a gun," He thought to himself. His first stop was Wood Green, where he went to see one of his long-time employers, Marlon Dean.

"My Lord [Jamaican accent]". He greeted him with a hug that felt like a cold embrace, he only knew the guy as a killer.

"You just got out today mate, what brings you here? Shouldn't you be laying low?" Marlon said calmly. "I don't want you jeopardising my place of business so unfortunately, I have nothing to offer you," he added, speaking slowly with a smile.

"I want some tools, mate. You owe me that much," Idi retorted after about a minute of silence."I don't owe you shit," Marlon said explosively."Based on our history of loyalty in business, why not?" he asked calmly, after going from one hundred to zero with his emotions.

They concluded their conversation after Idi negotiated his demands.

On August 29th in the summer of 2009 (ten years ago), Julius woke up around six in the morning. He needed time to acclimate and prepare for the long day ahead. He prepared himself some strong coffee for breakfast. He then freshened up, got his gun, and then left his flat in Forest Gate. He was dressed in a grey Adidas tracksuit with orange stripes that ran down the sides and trainers. Caron Parker worked on Wood Street. He waited diligently until 5 in the afternoon for when she would leave her office to go home.

She was a voluptuous and beautiful dark-skinned woman who knew how to dress and carry herself in a womanly fashion, especially on workdays. She was always promptly on time for work, and she was the first one to leave. He approached her as she made her way to the bus stop to go home. She knew who he was but was puzzled as to why he was watching her.

"C'mon Julius, please." she pleaded for him to believe her."You know what am looking for and you know you can't leave until I have it."

She trembled beneath his knees as he pointed the gun at her. He had no intention of using it, but she did not know that. She was alarmed and feared for her life.

The motorway was busy as they made their way directly under the bridge of the motorway, overseeing the train tracks in Leytonstone. Julius began to lose patience, so he upped the stakes. He pulled the trigger back and extended his arm with the gun.

"Idi's stash. I know you know where it is. You two have that Bonnie and Clyde thing going on, so I'll ask you once more: Where?" He shouted, with so much emphasis that he forgot to keep the gun in check. Julius shot Caron directly in the head, killing her instantly. He ran to his car and sped off, his heart racing. He had killed before, but he had never killed a woman, or anyone by mistake like this.

Sonny kept talking. As usual, his mouth was restless, and Idi did not want to hear him speak anymore. He was eager to get this business exchange over and done with. He just wanted to collect the money in exchange for the drugs in the boot so then he could disappear and not hear Sonny utter another word. Sonny was the driver while Julius was running an errand for Marlon. Things were going well as he started the day by having sex with his main girl, Caron. It always put him in a positive mood and gave him a personal high that always gave him comfort as he worked through the day.

A police car approached them in Stratford. He was puzzled, but routine and protocols convinced him to forget his thoughts and stay calm. Unfortunately, Sonny had had some cocaine that morning which left him in an even worse mood, especially in the sight of the approaching officer.

"Idi Isiah, could you come out of the car please?" The officer asked, speaking through a loudspeaker.

He complied and they retreated closer to the officer's car as they spoke. Sonny continued to sweat, given the unpredictability of the situation.

"Don't worry, this stop has nothing to do with you. However, we have some bad news about your girlfriend. We decided to get in touch because you conveniently drove past, and you are listed as her contact in case of emergencies."

"C'mon, officer, let us hear it," Idi replied after the officer's long introduction to their conversation.

"Caron has been involved in a homicide," he said calmly. "I will let you go but should you think of any information, here is my card. Please let me know."

He walked him back to the car only to notice Sonny's demeanour. He had been sweating and had a stench of paranoia about him.

The officer became suspicious. He decided to search the car and discovered a key of cocaine, a pistol, and a sawn-off shotgun.

THIRTEEN

December 20th, 2019 (present-day)

"A blast from the fucking past!" Kane said in a loud and vulgar tone.

"What did you say, honey?" Amani replied in reaction to his outburst, thinking that Kane was talking to her from afar.

"Sorry hun, Arsenal is losing, that's all," he replied in a jovial tone.

He resumed his wonderment. He had thought long and hard about his enemies and concluded that he had a small handful.He then thought about Julius's enemies and could hardly keep them to ten fingers.However, there was a situation that stood out that had his mind screaming for revenge.

47

He recalled one particular time that Julius had spoken about, a moment that had changed him and his life trajectory, as it had haunted him every day since it had taken place. In his mind, Julius was a crooked criminal but a criminal with a code. He felt remorse after killing Caron as he saw her as innocent. What made things more complicated is that he had killed the lover of someone he did business with, and they had the same boss.

Marlon knew that Julius was not to be trusted, and he had him followed and watched constantly. He never trusted him, but Julius was a good worker and highly effective, hence the reason he kept him on his payroll. However, considering Julius' recent growth of conscience after killing Caron, he decided that he was of no use to him, subsequently making it known to Idi that Julius was the one that had killed his girl 10 years ago. Unfortunately, Idi had been brought up on charges before he could act on his revenge — until now. Julius knew that Idi was a problem but after his incarceration, he had never seen him as a threat until it was too late. Kane did not want to make that mistake.

Idi was sloppy. He knew he was still alive by luck. He had been shot on the outside of his shoulder but fortunately for him, it was a flesh wound. He made his escape to an abandoned building in Victoria Park where they found an old club gym. There he found some old clothes to pressure the wound until the blood began to clot. He made his way back home where he sewed up his skin to close the wound, and then used some dressing from a first aid box he had found in the gym.

"I need your help and based on our history, you owe me big time, so do this for me and we are even. Otherwise, I will kill you and that is a promise, Sonny!"

Sonny had been out of prison five years before, but he knew Idi would come knocking one day. Therefore, he kept his mouth shut and did as commanded because he was scared. Idi knew that if he pressed him hard enough, Sonny would fold instantly, being the coward that he was. That was their secret, but everybody gave him the time of day because of his boss, Marlon. Idi didn't care and Sonny knew it.

"Sure, of course. Whatever you need," he pleaded with Idi, who was fuming.

"Oh yeah and Sonny? We need manpower," Idi said with a grimace.

Idi got Sonny's contact number from Marlon and within minutes of speaking with Sonny, he found out where Kane lived. On the day of Kane's release from the hospital, he stayed waiting outside his house, counting on the fact that Kane didn't know what he looked like. However, he did not know that Kane knew about Sonny through Julius and that Sonny's reputation of being a coward preceded him. Sonny was a coward, but he had a lot of bona fide gangsters and killers around him. He could be particularly useful which was the only reason Idi kept him alive.

"He'll live, for now," he admitted to himself, knowing he was just itching to blow Sonny away. He still blamed him for getting arrested. Sonny did not have him locked up, but he did inform Idi. He saw that as the logic for Sonny only receiving a five-year sentence, whereas he had had ten whole years taken from his life.

Sonny knew too much, and he was too weak to keep his big mouth shut. Cold and calculating, like a chessboard, Idi devised his plans several steps in advance.

FOURTEEN

Wednesday, December 25th, 2019. Christmas day was positive. Despite the onset of the prevailing issues that had followed him the past few weeks, he was determined to forget his issues and allowed himself to enjoy the day, if only for the sake of Amani. Amani took the day off. She was not a true believer in the Bible, but she respected the whole idea of Christmas being family-oriented. For the past five years, she had taken the night off to spend the day with her man. She arrived home feeling great and looking great — she was a beautiful soul in and out. Kane was mesmerised and continued to watch her as she arrived outside his mother's house and exited the car. She spoke aloud to her father on the phone about her mother, while entering the front door. It showed that she came from a close and well-knit family.

However, that was not what was on Kane's mind. Ever since he had taken over his mother's business a year ago. It was a residential care business that she had run for the greater part of her mature years coming up to 25 years total, she had decided that she wanted to retire and lead a different life. As always, he liberated her and encouraged her to look after herself and put her health before anything. But it was around this time that she had been diagnosed with an advanced stage of cancer and told that she had little time left to live. Impressively, she died five years after, which was a true testament to her strength and character. She fought all the way. It was not pretty but it was her way and all she knew.

Conveniently, as Amani entered the door, her conversation ended, when she saw Kane. The atmosphere changed between them, and he seductively approached her. She read between the lines and knew what he had in mind. They played their intimate game of resistance, mostly on her part, but eventually, she welcomed him in. They teased, licked, and tasted each other. He undressed her, caressing, and rediscovering all he classed as special about her, which was everything. She waited eagerly as he teased her, and he waited just enough until she erupted. His penetration was immense, and she sensed it all over her body as he played inside her, and she screamed with desire for more. She climaxed for the second time as they continued to change and interchange, savouring every moment of their special time.

Her beautiful body was tight and there was a solid and tense connection between her legs as he lifted her up and back inside, opening her wider and wider as she motivated him to put all of himself inside her until they both broke down and gave into a synchronised moan and climaxed together. They kissed for a minute before falling asleep without changing position.

Kane woke up to a reign of destruction as bullets exploded from outside and into the house. He instantly covered Amani as he urgently gathered himself and pulled down her to the floor, waiting for whoever was shooting to stop. They continued their assault on Kane's mother's house for a minute before disappearing into a black sprinter van. Kane urgently began to assess Amani, trying to check if she was hurt. Amani had been hit in the arm by one of the bullets. Kane was fuming in anger with himself at the thought that he had risked her life by bringing danger her way. The bullet appeared to have damaged her artery as she was bleeding profusely.

He did not hesitate, and he rushed her to the hospital, which took them about 15 minutes. When they arrived, Amani was losing consciousness, so he shouted for a doctor until he got someone's attention. He did not know how he would have continued living if anything had happened to her. He closed his eyes as tears built up as he tried to bear the contempt, remorse, and anger that he felt inside in a simultaneous eruption.

On Thursday at 6 am. Amani woke up and regained consciousness. She smiled as she caressed Kane's face. Kane did not wait for approval or resistance. He took Amani and disappeared from the hospital before anybody even noticed they were missing. He took her to her dad Benjamin's house. Her mom Elle-Ameen started to cry as soon as she saw her daughter, but the anger was apparent. Benjamin was full of it but composed, nonetheless. Elle-Ameen and Benjamin helped her inside, and Kane thought that they had entered a haven, so he tried to calm down. Kane was in shock. He tried to speak and even forced himself but every time he attempted to utter a word; he began to break down at the sight of what had become of the love of his life.

Elle-Ameen's past years of nursing had come in handy. She was always prepared as a result of the years of her husband's warring escapades, due to him being from a criminal background. She attended to her daughter's de-stabilizing condition, as her pulse was becoming weaker. Elle-Ameen understood the situation and how to make her better; she was automatic in her response, and everything happened like clockwork when it came to handling Amani's condition. Kane and his father-in-law had issues coping. They remained shocked at the thought that it was someone so close to them having such complications in their life, at the onset of her appearing to develop further health problems. But hey were reminded how strong she was by her pulling through. This was one of the reasons why Kane had admired both mother and daughter, and mutually, her father shared the same feelings. Elle-Ameen made Amani stable again, she went back to sleep, and they watched over her for the first hour. They were all so focused on her that it appeared that time itself even stood still.

FIFTEEN

Kane stared down the barrel of the pistol aimed at his head. Alarm bells were ringing, a prime indication of him appreciating the magnitude of the situation.

"You promised me that my girl would always be safe, and you lied. Give me one reason I shouldn't kill you right here and right now?" Benjamin spoke calmly but he was stern.

"I will kill the people responsible for this. I'll accept whatever you think is best after I am done." Benjamin's body language indicated that this was not his first time pointing his gun with intent, so Kane knew that he had to speak with caution as one wrong word may have him killed. His family was what Benjamin lived for, and what he would die for should the situation call for that precise act.

Benjamin was serious and rightfully so, for his daughter was in bad shape and he held only one person accountable.

Kane was surprised at his level of composure in front of the gun, but he now realised that he would never be the same again. Ever since his mother had passed away, it was almost like losing a part of himself. It numbed him to the point that he welcomed death, except when he was with the only other person that he truly cared for, who was now in critical condition. He intended to make it right.

Kane did not love to fight but he knew how to. His father, Dane, had made sure of that. He had been a boxer since the age of 10 years old up to his 18th birthday when he quit. He was a true talent, but he did not want to pursue it. Kane and Dane's relationship had fractured because of his actions; his father saw everything as disrespect to him.

Kane and Benjamin figured out their issues and the hostility began to lift from the room. The door was shut, and they were isolated, as this was a debate between two men that warranted no interruptions. Benjamin spoke anonymously[ominously]; he was organising an attempt to prepare to rectify the situation in reaction to his daughter and her current condition. As he intended to retaliate, he felt obligated to make sure that his family could never be hurt again by those responsible. He was deep in thought. It was clear that this was not his first situation where he had the intention of engaging in serious violence, and he knew the people who would help him to carry out his actions, judging by his conversations on the phone.

Within an hour, a black sprinter van parked outside the house, and Kane wondered who Benjamin really was. They made their way outside the house and greeted the men. Kane was on guard as Benjamin instructed him to enter the black van. Four black men with machetes and shotguns appeared as the van doors opened. The machetes had dried blood on them.

Four Rastafarians. Kane knew they were killers. He had seen that look before. Their intent was beyond apparent, but he didn't know whether to welcome their ride-along or to prepare for his demise. Either way, he was destined to find out. There was nothing distinctive about them. They were tall but slim, slender but strong, and even their clothes were low-grade to the point that they could be mistaken for homeless people. However, one thing that they could not change was the look in their eyes. He knew what killers looked like.

They rode quietly in the back of the van — everybody had bad intentions on their mind. They all knew that this day could be their last. Benjamin and Kane decided to look in the last place they expected to find their enemy, surmising that the best place to start their search was Sonny's house. Once again, Kane was at an advantage because of Julius and for that he was grateful. Julius knew Sonny's whereabouts due to him being affiliated with the same criminal organisation years back. He was counting on Sonny's lack of ability to be tactical and smart about his movements making him predictable to find. They made their way to locate him. However, he knew that Idi was not that stupid, and would not make it easy.

They drove past Sonny's house. They had been watching his house for over 12 hours without a whiff or hint of his presence. Eventually, Kane and Benjamin broke in. They didn't know where he could be, but this was no surprise as they knew how to stay low. An hour later, they wrapped things up and decided to take a drive back to Kane and Amani's house, have something to eat, and regroup.

When they arrived, driving towards the house, nostalgia kicked in. Kane decided to view his home from afar on the approach, and he experienced flashbacks and euphoric moments of when his woman was well, a long time before the current problems had started. His thoughts were suddenly interrupted by another nagging feeling as he noticed a car that he had seen before. He could not quite remember or place his suspicions until he saw Sonny aiming a shotgun through the car window. Benjamin began evasive manoeuvres as he approached Sonny in the car with the gun. At this point, there was no going back as Benjamin had already decided to commit even if it meant his death.

Sonny randomly shot at the car in a panic as the big van approached. Benjamin's intentions were to destroy both cars in the collision. Both parties began shooting and the bullets started ricocheting, causing casualties. Benjamin was shot, two of the dreads in the back died on collision and the others were injured. It was an execution that took three lives, and both cars were also destroyed, with Sonny inside dead on impact. Idi stood, stunned by the lengths that they had gone to. He had planned it perfectly, tracking Kane for hours ever since they had infiltrated Sonny's house. It was only by chance that he had driven away in his car and saw their approaching black van. Kane and Benjamin watched from afar and waited for their opportunity.

"That useless shit," Idi cursed about Sonny as he spat on the floor and ran to his car across the road, knowing the convenience of his death for he planned to kill him either way. He never anticipated that this would be the result but he murmured what he had concluded, "Only Sonny could fuck up a good plan."

Kane was shooting his semi-automatic. It ripped through the street to the point that Idi turned around and ran to the house. Idi kicked the door in and disappeared, and Kane pursued him.

Kane entered the house apprehensively. He knew Idi was waiting to ambush him on his entry into the house but he could not stop himself; he wanted it to end today once and for all, irrespective of the cost. He needed to make amends. He was aware that Idi had dropped his gun on the way in, so he knew he had the advantage.

Idi felt vulnerable without his gun to defend him, but he decided that being shot was not an option. He waited behind the door and surmised that it was not the best plan. He felt that it was the least expected action for him to take, and he had nothing to lose.

Idi grabbed Kane's hands from behind the door as he pointed his gun out upon his entry into his home. He managed to fire one shot that ricocheted off the steel table and into the window that had been recently replaced. Idi managed to subdue Kane and pushed the gun away from them as they struggled, knowing that he had his knife on him. He intended to use it and put Kane down once and for all. Kane anticipated as much.

Idi pulled his knife out in a slashing fashion to try and cut Kane. He was not successful. Kane anticipated this. He grabbed Idi's hand, the one that was holding the knife, and turned it. He now had him in a bear hug as he brutally pulled the knife toward him and Idi's chest. They struggled for what seemed like a lifetime for Benjamin, but he waited because he felt Kane needed to handle the issue on his own. In his mind, this was a test to show that he could do what needed to be done.

The immense screaming from within the house as they fought came to an abrupt halt. It suddenly got quiet before there was a sharp pulling open of the door; Kane emerged. Cut and bruised, he looked shocked at what had just taken place, for he had taken Idi's life.

He knew that things could have gone either way between them as they fought, and despite the many fights he had been in, this had been the first time that he had ever taken a life.

Benjamin instinctively shook his head in approval.

SIXTEEN

December 25th, 2025

Kane helped Amani out of the car. She struggled as she tugged and pulled to get herself out of the car, then she worked hard to find her footing to balance her stance. She felt amazement at how things had changed, especially since they had come so close to death over the years. She was grateful that the only issue she was bothered with now was the change involving her body, bearing in mind that she was seven months pregnant and was expecting sooner rather than later. In her mind, it was "scaring the shit out of her" as she had reiterated over the past few months. However, she remained grateful since Kane and her family had been there as she recovered from her life-threatening situation. Kane and Benjamin had become closer over the years, bonding over wanting to protect Amani.

Life for Kane and Benjamin had been peaceful, and they remained grateful but on guard, unwilling to retire as pandemonium seemed to occur when it was least expected.

They made their way to a celebratory meal with Amani's parents, a tradition that they now consistently practiced every Sunday. Fittingly, on this occasion, it was also Christmas Day, which they considered to be a time of family appreciation.

They were slow in their preparations to leave home but that had become common recently, Amani complained as she struggled to find decent-sized clothing to wear due to her predicament; she blamed Kane and cursed the day she met him. Kane did not take notice. He knew that she was constantly trying to push his buttons and he was in too good of a mood to play her games. Plus, he was contemplating the journey that he had taken over the last few years and he was feeling grateful for his accomplishments and the life he now got to see as the calm before the storm. However, if anybody were to ask what storm? He would retort, "Fuck knows."

Kane and Amani arrived to hear the drama between Benjamin and their mother as they argued over trivial issues, about something in the past that had happened to them in the 90s.

"Hello there, Mrs-." Kane was interrupted.

"I told you to stop with this 'Mrs.' a long time ago, Kane. You have been part of this family for far too long. I'm putting my foot down," Elle-Ameen complained.

He had always respected Amani's mother and loved her dearly. He always saw her like a queen, and she carried herself as such, so he always referred to her by her title — until now.

"Apologies, Mrs. Elle-Ameen," he joked.

"Hardhead, but you're getting there," she retorted.

It was a merry day indeed, and it showed how tight and close-knit the family had become over the years. Benjamin and Elle-Ameen knew that Kane did not have much time for his father and so they appreciated him being so respectful to them and their daughter. Because of this, they always treated him as family and appreciated the care he showed. They perceived it to be a special relationship.

Kane excused himself as he retreated to the bathroom. He admitted that he was aware that the relationship between him and his father was not the greatest and never would be, but he still felt responsible for checking in and showing his respects when the occasion demanded, knowing that his father appreciated it.

"Howdy," Kane said into the voicemail but before he could continue, his dad answered.

"Everything good?" Dane replied in a surprisingly pleasant tone.

"Everything is good. Just showing my respects and making sure you're still in one piece" Kane expressed.

"A lot of people have been doing that around you recently, have you ended up not being alright?" He was referring to Kane's now past years of violence.

Kane went quiet, having felt the urge to cut the conversation short.

"Thanks for looking out for me Dane. I am glad you care," Kane said sarcastically.

"Right, I mean, I am your dad, after all," Dane pleaded in a not so calm tone.

"Are you?" Kane retorted before hanging up abruptly.

He admitted that his dad knew how to push his buttons with his righteous, judgmental... He stopped his thoughts, calmed himself, hung up, and returned to the living room.

Amani welcomed him with open arms and a kiss. Her parents had already retired to their bedroom for the night.

As usual, Amani could read her man like a book, and she could sense the annoyance from the look on his face. She knew that Kane usually checked in with his father on days such as these; usually with a smile on his face as he would leave the best until last, which would be his final call to his mother. This was because his dad would usually leave him feeling frustrated, then his mom would calm him down. On this occasion, Amani felt that it was her responsibility to keep him balanced and positive on a day that they both devoted to being family-oriented.

Amani and Kane prepared for their departure from Amani's parent's house. They suddenly felt the need to be alone in their domain, so they were brief with their goodbyes before getting into Kane's car. It was night

61

and it was approaching 11:30 pm. They quietly departed. Their mood was pleasant yet tranquil; thus, they made their way home.

Seventeen

Kane was in his head through their journey, thinking vividly about his last quality time spent with Amani. They're on route to attend a meeting; organised by Benjamin on their initial departure from their family safe house. He pondered specifically on the night before with his beloved. It was beautiful, Kane could still taste Amani in his mouth; the aroma of pleasure still lingered in his clothes. They had started by making love to each other on their very arrival to their bedroom. The love was immense between them, leaving no stones unturned. Kane tasted Amani, the pleasure was reciprocated as they enticed each other, going from one position to the next, they were thorough in their need to satisfy one another, and their lovemaking only grew in passion as the time passed by.

Amani then began to reveal to Kane that she had planned the enticing occasion by finally revealing her sexy lingerie; a dark purple bra and panties, an all-access situation making Kane smile, even more so as the outfit showcased her amazing body underneath. Kane took pleasure in being thorough, he wanted to savour every moment of what he felt was everything special about her. He had her stand still while he rotated around her, all the time kissing her waist. As he approached her from the back, she took a deep breathe in suspense of the surprise Kane would find in realising she had nothing connected to the panties protecting her modesty from the back. He smiled, and she started to relax again knowing the silence was one of admission that he was loving the moment. He remained in constant awe of her in moments like these as she always knew how to surprise him in a pleasant way. They simply concluded with their foreplay. Amani and Kane had thrust each other into what was one of the best nights of their life. He still smiled, watching every action over and over in his mind's eye.

It was dawn, the sunlight slowly began to sweep the land, shining as it came out of hiding from beyond, lifting the shadow from across the land, revealing everything green. A vast plain with marked football pitches. The air was unforgiving as winter had started to settle in. Though for some reason, the situation didn't appear as climaxing as it was supposed to be, at least for Kane and Benjamin, as they arrived outside Kingsmead Park by taxi, where Benjamin had reinforcements waiting for him. Kane and Benjamin wished they had at least packed some gloves before their initial departure as they rubbed their hands – indicating how cold their surroundings were – and walked over to the specific location where they had everybody waiting for them.

In their current stance they looked ahead, in sight of Jimmy with five men accompanied by 'mean mug' expressions on their faces. At first, Kane thought the men were ready to hurt somebody, but eventually, the closer he approached, he realised they were just really cold. They dressed in all-black clothes, hoodies, and black hats – coincidentally like a form of uniform, an indication of how ready they were to go to work. They stood composed despite the signs their body language was depicting. The men immediately embraced Benjamin and Kane on their approach, Jimmy was his usual self, the always upbeat character that he was, the weather never bothered him one iota.

"Uncle Benjamin!" Jimmy called out, coming directly into Benjamin giving him a warm embrace.

"Big son" Benjamin said with a smile, he had time for Jimmy, so his affections were reciprocated in full.

They took a moment to catch up and converse. Benjamin went over and spoke with the men accompanied by Jimmy, then took some time and explained what the plan was. However, Benjamin's first intention was to get some supplies for him and Kane from Tottenham, where Kane's mom's house still resides. They soon departed and Kane and Benjamin were driven in Jimmy's Range Rover.

The mood stood still in the car; Kane got the chance to have more of a look at the people he was making his journey with. He saw the signs, nothing he hasn't seen before, but it still tells a tale every time he notices the cold and callous nature of individuals that are in the line of work with Jimmy and his men. They carried a soldier's demeanour like it bore a weight, speaking as little as possible, only speaking when spoken to the majority of the time. Though there wasn't much to be spoken about when your actions are supposed to speak for themselves. The men had such cold eyes, and though they appeared quite used to their situation (as the ways they had of disarming themselves with their words expressed), there was still that all-apparent body language to remind you of their true nature; that at the flip of a coin, they could shoot you in the face without a second thought. It is quite a situation seeing somebody being buried six feet deep as Kane had seen with Idi, but that thought brought a warmth to his core, and suddenly he felt more in the mood to do something ever cruder, so he welcomed whatever crooked plan Benjamin had in mind.

EIGHTEEN

They arrived at their destination. Kane stood tall at the front of the house in Haringey where his mother house lived. The morning was vacant, not a person in sight, considering how early it still was. A feeling of euphoria washed over him, such feelings he found rare, but he relished it either way. Benjamin exited the car with Jimmy still inside and with his men, silent with their nonchalant appearance, in the back. Kane and Benjamin went inside to go and collect whatever they felt may be needed to execute their plan.

"What's that sound?" Kane thought he heard a racket outside.

In the meantime, Jimmy was waiting in the van with company, armed to the teeth. Consequently, they fell into a state of relaxation, simply waiting to go find trouble. Jimmy went to the side of the house to go pee as he was bursting to go since before the initial meeting. He shouted to his friends, "Soon come back!" as he walked off in a hurry to the enclosed side of the house.

Ignorant to the approaching car, creeping slowly. The lights purposefully switched off, using the still shade and lacking sunlight as an advantage. Suddenly, the car stopped parallel to the black Range that still had Jimmy's men in the back.

The windows were tinted, so it was no coincidence that Jimmy's men had no knowledge of what the opposing car's occupants were about to do. It was simultaneous, as the creeping car's windows came winding down, exposing just enough of the gun to aim, they started shooting. The constant spitting of bullets had shells raining down on the floor between the two cars. Jimmy came to his senses, opening his eyes, realising the situation – it was too late, for everybody in the car was dead on-site. However, that didn't stop him from pulling out his own gun and letting off shots from over the wall that stood in front of Kane's mother's house. It was not the most strategic move, but he was livid, and he emptied his pistol with everything he had towards the car. He thought he may have wounded one of the men in the car, but his efforts just resulted in gathering the attention of the whole crew of shooters in the car. They reloaded and began to focus on Jimmy, the wall almost began to shiver, as it became brittle with the bullets spraying into it. They aimed to destroy Jimmy on the approach, as two of the strangers left their car to get closer to Jimmy.

Kane and Benjamin were in the house making preparations and packing their weapons. Benjamin went into his bag and pulled out another weapon. It was dark so it took Kane a second to see exactly what it was Benjamin had in his hand. Kane jumped with surprise in reaction to the size of the gun Benjamin was holding – such a vigorous reaction that he almost pulled the trigger of the hand pistol he had in his hand, nearly shooting himself in the foot. It was an AK-47, it was the first time Kane had seen one, and his body language showed as much.

Benjamin led Kane downstairs, and they both looked out of their individual windows, astonished at what they are witnessing. Benjamin and Kane didn't ponder their actions as they fired without hesitation through the window, spotting that Jimmy was about to get overrun with bullets as the men approached the house. Kane and Benjamin shot to kill, firing bullets at them without a second thought in an effort to save Jimmy's life. They turned their attention towards the car and continued to stream bullets into its side. Kane had a pistol, so he was more strategic with his targeting. He aimed at the petrol tank. One of the men realised what the situation was becoming, with the integrity of the car now being compromised. The stranger jumped from the car, leaving the rest of his company to contend with the explosion, the men dying instantly as the car exploded.

Kane and Benjamin ran over to the stranger and apprehended him before he could even think to react after the explosion and make his escape. He was a small man in height, but with a big gun; on their approach he jumped towards the gun to protect himself, but it was too late for they were already at his throat. His face was not exposed as he wore a black fitted mask. At this point his identity was of little concern to Kane and Benjamin, they were more focused on the apprehension of him to gain more information and answers. Benjamin made a mental note to make sure not to let Kane kill the stranger before he could get all the answers he needed. He had noticed over a short period now Kane's temperament had changed, becoming trigger happy and somewhat of a hot head.

On their approach Benjamin didn't hesitate, he knocked him right between his eyes with the butt of the long weapon that he was using.

They wasted no time in disappearing out of town in Kane mother's car, which still resided on the side of the road around the corner. It occurred Kane that he had not come to terms with the situation pertaining to his mom's death, certain aspects of his mom's death. He suddenly found himself contemplating over the thought of selling his mom's car, and even her house; the emotional conflict stirred inside, and so he swallowed the thought and got out of his head in effort to escape his mind.

An hour later they arrived back at the cornfield on the outskirts of London, in the direction of Bedford, at the broken-down shed where they sorted their last dispute. The man was tied up in the trunk of the car, they took pleasure in letting him out especially for what they had in mind for him – considering he had just tried to shoot their heads off. However, Benjamin decided to be tactical, for this was a dangerous game of brute outcomes, a process of finesse. He also didn't want to waste the opportunity to get some answers. He instructed Jimmy to take the guy inside where they may still be able to talk business in private, in the absence of prying eyes. Jimmy didn't hesitate, having a gift for being a brute on occasion, he couldn't wait to get started. Jimmy grabbed the small man with one hand, threw him onto his shoulder, and started walking. Slowly in anticipation, he conversed with the individual, he described this process as "giving a pep-talk" as he bragged about all the potential things that may happen to the stranger, running down a list of things he had in mind in his ear, all the while giving an effort to create suspense and tension. Jimmy knew that he would only be the warm-up, beating and brutalising him physically when the time comes, Benjamin would be the individual playing head-games and implementing the real tactics for mental torture.

Being a student of mental warfare, Benjamin was primed in the art of intimidation.

In the meantime, Benjamin and Kane spoke briefly outside, Benjamin loved the ruthlessness of Kane when the occasion took him, but he only requested one thing from Kane.

"Control your anger son, don't lose yourself in your pain."

His words resonated with Kane, more to the point, he recognised the fact that Benjamin had called him son for the first time; it was almost an acknowledgement that he was starting to see him as more of a family member by the day. Benjamin's words spoke volumes. At this point he had a thought to embrace the need to express himself about his pain. However, given the time and place, perhaps another time – to a professional – would suffice, or better yet, to his women, for she always steered him in the right direction. All these thoughtful solutions, he only hoped he'd remember to act upon them should he make it through this period of trials he was experiencing. Kane tried to recompose himself, he knew Benjamin was right, and he very much wanted to remain balanced within the overall situation; he thought it necessary if they were going to make it out alive.

And just like that, Kane appeared calm, as if he found his mind and his sense of logic again. He and Benjamin made eye contact, then Kane went about nodding in acknowledgement that he was fine, and so they carried on. Kane stayed at a distance, he wanted to give Benjamin some space to let loose with whatever he had in mind. It was like clockwork, Benjamin started to really enquire at the stranger.

"I'll ask this once, who sent you?" he spoke sternly into the side of the individual's face. Meanwhile, Jimmy was busy putting in work on the stranger's kneecaps, he was relentless; he had nails, scissors, pliers and all the essentials a professional would need for such an occasion. While Benjamin went about questioning. It was almost like they were gradually building up, and Kane wondered what was going to happen next. Though things got less unpredictable as it appeared Benjamin was looking less like his 'cool as Kool-Aid' self. His voice started to strain, agitated and somewhat off balance for some reason. Kane requested to speak with Benjamin, and Benjamin reassured Kane that he was fine – but his demeanour was not indicating what he was trying to insist with his words. Immediately, he went back to continue with his methods, followed by questions. Suddenly, Benjamin pulled out his gun and started shooting at the legs of the stranger, he started with his kneecaps, and the stranger replied by screaming. It was an antithesis of what was supposed to happen, even Jimmy was surprised, as he was still going strong with the shooter tied to the chair, his tweezers and pliers in hand, about to pull on his toenails. He jumped when Benjamin started to shoot the legs of the stranger.

"Ben!", Kane was wilding out as the guy was on the floor crying out loud, unfortunately they were in the middle of nowhere with nobody to hear them. Though it made it less a concern to the surrounding party that something was not quite right with Benjamin. He finally responded to Kane. He turned and looked at Kane, he had a look on his face, and Kane knew that blood thirsty look so well. He took the gun and walked Benjamin out the room to ask what was going on, though he could guess, he asked Jimmy to take over in the meantime. Jimmy was puzzled and wanted to know exactly what the issue was also, plus Benjamin had been there for him so many times over the years – but he stayed and did as Kane requested. They walked outside the broken-down place to the front as the stranger continued to scream and cry tied up on a chair with Jimmy and his pliers going at his knees.

"Am not cut out for this anymore Kane, am getting too old for this dammit!", Benjamin said as he shrugged his shoulders, "There is something not right with me ever since things started to get bad for my family. I've been driven by anger for so long that I feel like it had started to burn me out, it dawned on me ever since the time my daughter lost her baby, while I held my wife unconscious hand in mine, thinking it wasn't supposed to be this way". Kane was surprised at the depth at which these words were expressed from, he never knew Benjamin to feel so much and to express it to him of all people. Kane started to think he clearly underestimated the level of respect Benjamin has for him.

Nevertheless, Benjamin's words hit home for Kane. It appeared he had been driven by anger for so long that it was slowly burning him out; the situation with his family only exacerbated the state. He had a flashback to the day Benjamin held a gun to his head, but now they were so close, the irony he could not help but acknowledge. Kane never spoke a word until Benjamin had gotten everything off his chest; he then went about encouraging him, allowing him to pull himself to together, for Kane knew that he had a lot to deal with, and the level of loss had simply caught up to him. When Benjamin was ready, they went back inside, with the plan that Kane and Jimmy would take the lead.

They entered the shed to find a dead body, it appeared Jimmy had successfully recovered what they wanted to know, with his meticulous methods, and had proceeded to end the stranger's life. Jimmy was cleaning up and taking care of the body. Benjamin had made quite a mess, but fortunately they had already spread a bag over the ground anticipating the death of the shooter, as protocol would dictate. Although, the mess was a convenient one; the majority of the blood in addition to brain matter (from the head shot carried out by Jimmy) were on top of the bag spread whole along with the body.

Jimmy picked the body up, barely phased by the weight of the dead man. He walked to the back and exited through the door. At the back he found a shovel leant against the wall. Jimmy smiled at the convenience of the situation, thinking he would take the opportunity to be thorough, for he was simply going to discard of the body and go about his business.

Kane, Benjamin, and Jimmy soon departed from the hideout which they were using for torture and to discard of the man's body. After exiting from the shed, they burnt the wooden structure that stood, using spare petrol stored in the back of Jimmy's Range. Benjamin was looking like himself again, he was composed and once again somewhat poised. Kane was appeased nonetheless but could tell he was merely keeping his trauma in a certain space inside, like a bottle. Kane felt that in itself told him that he was not out of the game quite yet, but they better try and fix whatever issues they intended before they ran out of time. There were not many people Kane trusted to this degree, to the likes of Benjamin; on their journey, Kane pondered hard, "no offence to Jimmy, but he clearly doesn't know enough of him to fully trust in such volatile situation", he thought. But Benjamin's presence had made their current predicament all the better; he had and intended to be with them to see everything through, he tried to be positive about their current situation.

They made their way back to Milton Keynes with Jimmy who was quite excited; it appeared he had not seen Benjamin's wife in a long time, and he intended to show his respect and catch up with her. Kane could understand and approve of his respect in sight of how motherly and maternal she was as a woman to the younger generation, such as Jimmy or other men and the likes of Kane. Kane and Jimmy began to speak and really got to know each on their journey to Milton Keynes in the back of the Range while Benjamin drove, close to a two-hour journey. Kane's eyebrows went up after Jimmy expressed that Elle-Ameen was his extended cousin, making Benjamin technically his family. Jimmy couldn't tell, but that meant a lot to Kane, for it showed that there was a genuine motive to be loyal and be there for Benjamin and his family, which stands to reason that Jimmy was whom he portrayed himself to be, and not in any way pretentious. "Yes, Kane she is my Auntie which made Benjamin the 'odd Uncle'", Jimmy ended with a smile as he waited for his words to hit home, Benjamin turned his head to look from the side of his eye in reaction to Jimmy's words while Kane laughed out loud. The journey had been one which grew everyone closer together, and so they felt bonded, more like a family.

NINETEEN

Marlon grew restless, he would sit and reminisce on his past endeavours, then make comparisons to where he was in time; he would always finish his sentence with "in my younger days, everybody would be dead already". Contemplating on the fact that he had grown and matured over the years and became evermore so meticulous about the way he liked to go about punishing his enemies – especially the ones that took something precious from him, like family. He wanted to burn everything in sight as he saw red, anything that was attached in any way to Benjamin, and he wanted to for a long time now.

However, like years ago, he wanted to act slowly on his revenge; he wanted it to be out of the blue and from nowhere so Benjamin would wonder in pain and even in suspicion of his enemy; the inkling of doubt would still linger in the air like a paper cut to cause further misery. Though now he has grown impatient, he wanted blood here and now, after waiting for so long, who could blame him for deciding on the callous actions he had been carrying out recently. Still calculating, but with even more so of a venom. The targeting of not only Benjamin's wife, but also his family, infiltrating his proximity, spilling the blood of the ones he held most dear to him. He watched him for so long, hearing news from various people that valued his loyalty over the years, and of course, he made efforts to ensure that he made Benjamin's business his concerns too.

Finally, he was distracted from his thoughts as one of his men approached with more information about the events that took place with the shooting in Tottenham outside

Kane's mother's house. He informed Marlon of the escape of Benjamin, Kane, and Jimmy, specially by their names. Marlon's mood changed; he began brooding. He couldn't bear the thought of Benjamin still breathing, it somewhat made his day more cloudy and unfulfilled. He was about to start cussing and complaining, although his man was not finished, he had more news. He informed Marlon that Benjamin and his people were being followed. He suggested that they had the means to finally put to rest everybody that Benjamin held dear, including Benjamin himself. They could finally be rid of him once and for all.

Marlon sat and pondered, he was unsure about the situation, it simply appeared too good to be true, but against his better judgement he was adamant to not let this opportunity be forgone, and not be tackled by chance. In fact, he intended to see this one through personally, he intended to look Benjamin in his eyes as he killed him slowly. Suddenly, his mind wavered back to the night he found out Logan had been killed, the depression he fell into, unbeknownst to anyone around him, for he kept everything to himself; in this business, a life of solitude was the best way he always went about situations pertaining to his internal issues, or anything relating to his emotions. That night he drowned himself in the alcohol. He drowned his sorrows in Hennessy that night and it made him somewhat numb to the ache where he bore the brunt of the pain from the loss of the son he never had; still he would admit, "he was a miserable fuck". Nonetheless, Marlon suffered dearly for Logan. On the night of his death, he sat in the middle of his office, by himself. The grief was piercing, and although he coped, for he was used to the passing of people, on this occasion, it was somewhat different – what with it being the passing of someone he saw so much as a son. He could confidently express that he fully went through a process of mourning in Logan's passing that nobody would have ever imagined. Though, the issues were always left unsaid, revenge consumed him, and for someone like him in this position, the only thing that would make a difference was the passing of the very person he felt was responsible – the passing of Benjamin was a must. At that point, he realised he had blacked out, forgetting he had his men waiting on his response with instructions on what orders he was to carry out, though he swiftly resumed the conversation; "I've made my mind up, get ready and tell them am coming along for the ride this time, am leading this mission". His thoughts were showing to be evermore unsettling, and he needed a clear head, so he decided to get some fresh air. Marlon took a walk to the back of his house; it was a surprisingly calming place that he never allowed anybody that he does business with to witness. He had the most peculiar and unexpected things in his garden; it appeared as though it was his place of relief, where he held his more therapeutic and remedial things that aided him in calming down. Marlon had a giant fish tank with sharks in it. On the other side he had another fish tank with fishes in it. He went over first to the fish tank and took fishes from there and fed the sharks. At first it didn't make a difference to his demeanour, but as he kept going, he started to unwind as if the tension of his mind started to release. Marlon picked up the phone and called to have a car come around the front for him. Within 10 minutes, he was making his way to meet his team that he had selected to support him on his quest for revenge.

James Dillon was his right-hand man. A big man by any measure; he stood at 6ft 4, 250 pounds. Strength was very obvious, and had the face of a monster, yet he always carried himself with a smile – as if that made him anymore innocent considering the number of lives he had taken for his boss over the years. He was Haitian born, long dreads and tattoos all over his arms, dark skinned so at times it camouflaged the fact he had so many tattoos. He had a big part to play in this mission they were about to embark on, and conveniently so, for they killed his brother who had been staying to watch over Sonny's house. So, he was also waiting to get his revenge on Benjamin for he knew he had everything to do with the death of his brother; he didn't know for sure if he pulled the trigger, shooting his brother in the head, but he knew somebody he was with was responsible. He was with Marlon when they had the call from his brother, and though nobody spoke on the phone, it spoke volumes that it was the last call he was ever going to make. It was at that point James Dillon's anger had been building, he had been savouring the call since he had heard from Marlon a while ago that he intended to make his move soon. Fortunately for him, the time was soon approaching, and he couldn't wait to handle his business. Along with him were another six men waiting at a distance while James and Marlon spoke on what the initial plan was. When all had been said between them, they went back to the other men to speak on what they had in mind. Marlon sat in comfort, for he didn't see the point of having a number two if he could lead, he ran his organisation like an army, therefore it was somewhat regimented. As expected, after painting the whole plan in the mind of the one man he trusted that could carry it out, he went about sitting and waiting as he waited for James to take the lead and explain to his men what the plan was and to what degree he expected them to play their part. He went about doing as expected, but at the end of his speech, he made it clear and explicit that whatever the situation, under no circumstance is Benjamin to be killed by anybody but Marlon or himself; to do so is to cause their own demise, and so the orders came with a certain venom that hit home with everyone. "The calm to the storm indeed", Marlon spoke out loud then started laughing hysterically, as all his worried were about to end over the weekend. Everyone was locked and loaded, weaponised and motivated to stay alive, so they listened as the words were spoken succinctly.

James Dillon wrapped up the conversation he was having with the men he was speaking with, then sent them on their way to occupy the vehicle at the back of the building, which was one of Marlon's safe houses they occupied. Marlon had a reputation of being a villain with all that that entailed, but to the individuals that worked around him, they have witnessed another side to Marlon at least once in a typical prolonged period of working for him. He was a leader, brutal in every sense for he didn't believe in rewarding incompetence. On the other hand, he rewarded good work ethic and initiative, and in his line of business he had found that these factors were such that breathed loyalty and respect for the people that surround him. While in other instances, there was an expectant level of fear for motivating people in the very way he would prefer them to be, but this was more so for individuals he considered his enemies. He sat pondering in his mind while he awaited James Dillon to come and brief him on any further details about the coming night, and at the same time he pondered about his enemy; Marlon felt a telling sense of destiny always putting itself between him and Benjamin, he thought further, then he pondered what it would be like if they never were enemies, for maybe they could have been great partners instead of good rivals. He brushed his thoughts off as Dillon approached him to speak more about the coming evening. He made a mental note to himself: he shall have to thank his ever so flashy friend for supplying him with the men, he was confident they would be more than enough to handle the issue at hand. At the end of his thought, James Dillon sat in front of Marlon at his desk, as usual; James Dillon's appearance was brutish and the mere thought of fighting with him was one that even proposed a challenge for your mental. Yet Marlon on many occasions such as this, would sit in front of men he found to be potentially formidable opponents (in the battling aspect) thinking how he would go about breaking him down; trying to find chinks in his armour, ways of causing efficient damage or inflicting pain in a worst-case scenario, or in the absence of a gun – for in that scenario, he would just shoot him dead without a second thought. James Dillon could read Marlon's thoughts as they sat in the split second before they initiated their conversation. He knew Marlon over a decade now, so he had gotten used to the many ways he like to sit and contemplate about individuals that may potentially be a threat one day, "and in some ways it is a blessing and curse", James thought, for in his mind it was a sign of respect for someone as formidable as Marlon is to be thinking of him as a threat; in their business it was a close as you could get to showing respect for someone, anything closer and that would be defined as love, and love would get you killed. In any respect, James appreciated the thought, on the other hand it could be a curse in the sense that he also respected Marlon, and there was always that potential that things could go bad. The relationship status between people changed like the weather, and he felt saddened by the fact he might have to kill him one day, but only because he knew he would not feel a way about breaking his neck without a second thought; no guns if he could help it, he deserved to die like a warrior on account of their history, and the fact he respected him that much. James was a thinker, and simply looking at him most people would not have guessed that about him, he was more a thinker than a strong man, hence the leadership he possessed amongst men. His brother was the person he first led from a young age, he was more known for his brawn, though most people would not guess that his biggest motivation for being the person he was, was all a consequence of his brother. He loved and idolised his brother, for James was held in such high regard not so much for his brutality, which he is fully capable of inflicting on individuals, but the fact that he was cerebral enough to get the best out of individuals, enemies, or foes, whether they wanted or not. Though his brother, younger, being less able, felt violence was the only way and consequently he was proactive and carried himself in such a way. But the fact remained that they were two different individuals, and the only thing they shared in terms of personality was their bloodline, for James Dillon was far more able.

"James, our friend came through for us again, it pays to have a rich fucker like him backing, make sure you shout him our respect on your return, he is pretty fond of you. By the way he was asking my permission to have you lead a few men for a job he got lined up to sort out a minor payback he needed to handle with some people back in North England, I told him it's okay with me but you should make the final decision on whether you're in or not", Marlon spoke with James, he showed him respect you would seldom observe, he knew James was the type of guy to appreciate and not abuse the type of relationship they shared without compromise.

James gave the nod in reference to the job enquiries by the anonymous, unnamed party mentioned.

"With that being said, I believe you should stay home today and let me go and handle the issue tonight, there is no need for you compromising yourself being in the proximity of a bloodbath, that's my job after all, and I'll add there is not certainty of what to expect, to that fact I feel we're somewhat going in blind." James spoke eloquently with Marlon, he gasped every time he heard James express himself to this degree, for the most part, he was a man of few words.

"Though I appreciate your concern old friend, this is personal, and regardless of the outcome I need to see this one through, this person has taken a great deal from me, it may be my ego talking, but I wouldn't be the man I am without seeing this one through personally".

At this point, James Dillon knew there was no convincing Marlon, but he could not shake the feeling that things could turn out to be unpredictable that night, for it was in a location out of his control, and these unpredictability factors made him uncomfortable. Nonetheless, these are the times when you earn the money you are paid. Thus, he felt he would have to rise to the occasion, ensure he planned accordingly, and make it his business to assure the safety of Marlon, whom he considered not only a friend, but it would also be practical; trusted employers were actually hard to find in this business. Finally, James Dillon and Marlon wrapped things up and made their way to make preparations before moving on to rally with the rest of their team. As per usual Marlon and Dillon appeared nonchalant, they were neither over excited nor under-stimulated, but ready to meet the occasion with the necessary aptitude required, although the anticipation was apparent. Everyone was, to an extent, trying to keep their suspense to a minimum.

Dillon followed Marlon outside to the back of the building where the rest of the men awaited their arrival in the van. Marlon of course had his car in front the van. As Dillon walked towards the van to accompany the men as they embarked on their journey, Marlon called for him to join him as he picked up his phone call; it was a mutual friend and ally they both are familiar with. Their flashy friend. He shouted out through the phone; "Yo, 'M'! How you like the new troops, they're some of my best, I hope they live up to your liking mate"

"No worries, mate, I can't say for sure if they're what you say, but we will soon find out" Marlon retorted.

"Okay my brother, if anything let me know when you return"

It was the evening, the sun was bare in the sky, about to make its escape. The sunset had a sinister glow about it, an extra red. Almost a prediction of the coming event that was about to take place.

James went on being the perceptive individual witness, as he stared from the passenger seat on the motorway. "How quaint" he spoke out loud.

Marlon thought he heard a ghost.

"Remind me to find out the definition of quaint if we make it through this James, knowledge is a shame to waste"
He said in a sarcastic and jokingly patronising tone.

James started to laugh.

He thought about explaining in detail what he was thinking but thought maybe it was best to show him.

"Look over there, doesn't the sunset look extra red to you"
"Not one bit mate, just another day, so stop smoking them trees and leave me alone as you sound high as fuck"

James laughed again.
He thought it prudent for Marlon to be so funny at a time such as the one they were in.

They chuckled for a few seconds then went back into focus, back into feeling the moment.
They drove quietly on their journey, conveniently as they both were comfortable around each other, there was no reason to force a conversation. The magnitude ahead was big enough, all they wanted to do was get a win, and that meant getting their revenge.

It was Easter Sunday, Benjamin and Kane were in their element, for they had their family under the one roof, and they wanted to make the day worthy for the occasion of being family oriented like the far away Christmas they had once before as a family. Kane and Amani had not got out of bed yet, as Benjamin and Elle-ameen were busy in the kitchen cleaning and setting the mood in the household for the very purpose they perceived would be a special one, in terms of quality time spent, they shared an intimate smile between each other, then began to discuss the past and their various escapades along with adventurous outings alone and not a care in the world. Kane and Amani looked at each other, they were so intertwined in the moment, there was nothing anybody could do to distract them. Amani tried to pin Kane down on the bed, Kane responded by flipping her over on her back, not a moment lost in their transition. Amani almost cried out in reaction to Kane thrusting himself deeper inside her; she wanted to scream. Though she knew their cover would be blown with their parents downstairs, thus, she bit Kane on the shoulder almost as a sign to share the level of intensity she felt in reaction to what he was doing to her. They carried on tussling and turning, always showing commitment to being creative, and inclined to never miss a moment to share a moment together in the name of lovemaking and celebrating what they saw as their unbreakable bond together. They had been caught up with each other for over an hour, and Kane smiled as he saw the signs, as her eyes started to roll backwards, and she finally climaxed; her body shivered, she let go and held nothing back as she moaned increasingly loudly, Kane covered her mouth in surprise.

"Babe you're going to wake the neighbours" Kane said in a soothing tone.

"What neighbours? We're in the middle of nowhere Kane!" Amani retorted to Kane. Suddenly they both started to laugh. They soon wrapped things up and went to clean up to go downstairs to join Benjamin and Elle-Ameen.

Kane made his way to their en-suite bathroom, Amani couldn't resist to slap him on the bum.

"You're going to pay for that" Kane said joking.

"You promise?" Amani replied cheekily.

"To be continued" Kane was getting in the mood for some banter.

"Okay Kane go shower will you" Amani spoke out loud, knowing her words would inflict annoyance, but they both were enjoying their back and forth.

As Kane got into the shower to wash off, she went straight in to join him. They continued for another in the shower. They arrived downstairs just in time for lunch as Elle-Ameen and Benjamin finally finished preparing an afternoon meal for everyone. Though Benjamin hardly moved from his chair during the whole process, he just sat on the cushioned seat and told stories thinking that his wife did not notice he was doing more talking than cooking; she knew him very well and usually would allow him to sit and stay in luxury, for she wanted to do everything for him. Elle-Ameen was a control freak in her own right and the only reason she had not been so demanding is due to the fact Benjamin had a stronger character, and her influence most times didn't work on him, though he admired her fire.

TWENTY

Kane and Amani entered the kitchen play fighting, it was a beautiful sight to see considering the turmoil of the situation they had all experienced recently that had not been totally resolved; however, situation called for them to live in the moment, and so they did their best to carry on and live life the best way they could. It was as if the room came alight for Benjamin and Kane to be sitting with their other halves looking so happy, for they could not totally switch off from their situation as they feared things had yet to escalate for the worse. Nevertheless, they enjoyed the moment, in the cosy and well decorated kitchen they sat, they had prepared enough food for a small feast. There were sweet potatoes, a formidable amount of fried fish with a salmon sliced laying on the side. An excess amount of greens, cabbage, and another pot of spinach, with cooked rice and peas with fried chicken. Neither of them were big eaters, but they needed to have a memory well decorated to ensure they remembered the times. Considering the onset of the morning, it was only fitting that things played itself out in such colours in relation to family ties and togetherness, for in a few hours there was a chance that things would never be the same again. Benjamin got up from the table as his phone started to ring, it was Jimmy.

Benjamin spoke hysterically "Jimmy where are you we're about to eat"

"Sorry Uncle Ben I met a lady last night and we had a few drinks, and you know..."

Jimmy smiled, even though Benjamin couldn't see his face he could sense the pause was due to him smiling as he relived only memories.

Jimmy continued "Am on my way back now"

Benjamin reserved his judgement for later, for he thought it reckless the level of impulsiveness Jimmy had displayed in such a random venture, especially with the situation being what it was. Though he knew Jimmy for being an individual that needed to blow off some steam from time to time, so he tried to relax and give him the benefit of the doubt even in this situation. He walked back into the room where everyone sat at the table waiting for his return, as they pondered what news awaited them now. Benjamin sat and didn't speak on anything, and so for a second the air lingered with a sense of unsettling, although they figured things are not as bad as his mood indicated, he was merely displaying his occasional broody persona.

Meanwhile, Jimmy was a couple miles down the road, making his way back towards the house in his Range, still laced with a few bullet holes in the side of the car; though nobody without the smarts and wisdom of the life they led would be able to surmise what situation could have led to a conclusion so specific that it resulted in holes in the car. He was in a good mood, he had still been excited from the sexual encounter he'd had in the early morning with a certain female that been giving the eye all night, and it was welcomed by Jimmy, for he so needed to blow off some steam while in the vicinity of female attention. He drove as his mind drifted in and out of the way his eventful night had gone, and it made him feel ever so much more excited and alive to the point that it dulled his senses to his current surroundings to a degree; for as he drove there was an approaching car from the back, it was creeping until it got close enough. Behind that approaching car there was another car following. Suddenly, both cars began to speed, and by the time Jimmy came to and realised the developing situation, things had already begun to escalate.

Both cars approached from either side of Jimmy. Shot guns aimed directly at the driver's position. They did not hesitate; Jimmy managed to get one shot off, directly shooting the head of one of the shooters with their heads out the blacked-out vehicle to his right. The shooter fell outwards towards the face of the Range, already dead a result of the head shot, and then on impact with the floor, as his head was caught between the wheels of Jimmy's car, he was no more. On the left side the other shooter managed to get a shot off, painting the side of Jimmy's Range with bullets. Jimmy was hit in the arm and leg, he started bleeding profusely. He instantly lost control of the car, and his Range ran into the car on his right as the driver still trailed with a second shooter in the back of the car looking to exit and move forward into the front seat to replace the shooter than had been killed. They trapped the Range, with Jimmy's lack of control and revving in pain, they were able to subdue the movement of the Range. Eventually, Jimmy's vehicle was stationary in the middle of the road, a few miles down from the house. At this point he had lost a lot of blood from the bullet wounds, as they crept towards the front to the car door, he was about to lose consciousness, though it didn't stop them gun bucking him with the long shot gun they were wielding in his face.

Jimmy woke up, writhing in pain, surrounded by enemies, it was as if things started to appear ever so darker for him. He smiled as he looked upon somebody he didn't quite know but he assumed (and assumed right) he did.

"Marlon, right?" Jimmy spoke out loud.

"I see you've heard of me" Marlon spoke with confidence. It had been a while but once in Beckton.

"Well looked what the cat dragged in James, we have a fan, and apparently my reputation precedes me" Marlon's men looked down on Jimmy with a fierce smile on their faces.

It was as if they were playing 'piggy-in-the-middle', and Jimmy was just about done being seasoned, and about to be put to be roasted.

He went to attempt to move, but suddenly all guns were spying his half dead body on the floor, waiting for an excuse.

James stepped in, "Wait not yet, we're in need of bait so he will be coming with us"

"Awe thanks mate, I didn't know you care" Jimmy retorted in response to James's instructions.

He then smiled, but James did not see the funny side of what Jimmy had to say; he took one of the shot guns from one of his men and knocked him to the head again, putting him back to sleep.

"This guy just can't get a break, can't imagine the headache" Marlon showed a callous sense of pity for his enemy laid out on the floor, he revelled in his misery, and the initiation of pain that they were putting him through.

Marlon had some of his men throw Jimmy in the back of his Range, they cared little about his life and the fact he was still bleeding, they knew his life was only convenient for the time being. Even Jimmy knew he was not living to tell the tale of the night, but he handled it like any person would with nothing to lose living the type of life he led for so many years; he embraced the pain and all that came with it. Marlon and his men were not satisfied by any means, and for them the night was only beginning. James and Marlon along with their eight men drove on to where Benjamin resided. They knew exactly where to find Benjamin and they had known his movements for a very long time now; unbeknownst to Benjamin and Kane, Marlon had made it his business to follow them since the day they decided to survey his place of work. He had made it his business to ensure he did his homework about his enemies after that noticeable situation with their attempt at camping outside his home for a prolong period. He was not one to miss out on the bigger picture of greater detail, especially when it came to an enemy and the way they operated. Still, it was no act of omniscience, for it was his friend, Flash, that had been the one that took notice of them from the beginning and made it their business to ensure Marlon was aware of the situation. It was convenience as he had already decided on the killing of the enemy that he had hated ever so much over the years and was unrelenting with his hate towards him. Moreover, he was well aware of Benjamin's return to London ever since the funeral, but he stayed despite their situation. At first, he was ignored, until James Dillon's brother was killed, at this point he could no longer bide his time in limiting his plans on the prolonged killing, at a later date, of Benjamin. James Dillon arrived at Marlon's house that day, he was blood thirsty, a result that was due to the demise of his younger brother, it had shocked, the passion and remorse James had shown that day, even though they were as friendly as their situation could allow over the years without compromising the dynamics of their relationship. Marlon understood and he could relate, James' feelings resonated very well with Marlon, for he could still sense the raw emotions still present within him at the times prior to the killing of his nephew Logan. Logan and James younger brother were of similar character, for they were both immature in a multitude of ways and it showed in their actions and the way they liked to go about doing the various, reckless practices they had gone about doing over the years. However, family was family, and despite how they may feel, the principle in this situation runs deeper than blood itself; after all, it was what separated them from the animals in both James and Marlon's eyes. Marlon was in a whirlwind of thoughts as he pondered, awaiting the timely arrival to Benjamin's location. He grew eager, and blood-thirsty himself, considering he had waited for this opportunity for a long time, so to see it coming to fruition had brought a sense of suspense in the form of salivation on his part, for he could not wait for the blood to start running for the deserving party. Finally, his nephew's name can have some respect on it, though overdue in thought of the time since his demise.

TWENTY ONE

Benjamin and Elle-Ameen had gone to bed in the early evening, and left Kane and Amani downstairs arguing. Whenever Amani and Kane get into their problems, laying afloat for the whole family to see, Benjamin and Elle-Ameen would usually make their exit from the overall issue, abating the emotional infliction that comes with bearing witness to the various issues. They did not wish to get drawn into their world, then having to choose sides between the two, for they were both seen as grown people and relationships are to be given the respect to not be interrupted, but at best seen from afar where Benjamin and Elle-Ameen are concerned.

As the Range came creeping down the road, closing in on the front door, it chuckled, and then some; a callous and cold sound, as Jimmy woke up from his slumber, he knew not where he was, but he had anticipated the whole team had just showed up at the safe house where Benjamin resided with his family.

Amani and Kane finally retired from their verbal conflict as it was starting to border on becoming explosive. Consequently, Amani decided to take a break and leave the house to get some fresh air at the back of the house, as she walked high-spirited out the back door, she missed she sound of the car that approached outside. Suddenly she started to cry, it was as like a few recent affairs had crept to the forefront as a result of her and Kane's dispute, for she hated dispute with her partner so much that it disturbed her to the core every time they had to go through one of their disagreements that escalated out of control. For the first time in a long time, she embraced herself and allowed herself to cry, then an unwavering feeling of loneliness washed over her; she contemplated on the thought that she had lost her baby, which she had failed to acknowledge, but could not be ignorant to the fact it had been hurting. Amani was hurting to the core, and the only person that could have helped her get through her situation, she constantly felt contempt for, and in certain instances, she wanted more to fight with Kane instead of finding solutions as of recently, which made her sad. She continued in thought for a while yet as she cried in acknowledgement of her pain at the loss of her child.

In the meantime, Kane was getting anxious, he sat on the sofa, twitching at every sound, attentive to every thought. He had succumbed to paranoia; similarly to Amani, he had felt bad for some of the exchanges he had with his her and it had hurt him as much as it had hurt her. Their arguments always had a chain effect on both parties, however the symptoms were somewhat different for the individuals that they were. Fortunately, for Kane, his situation made him heightened and more alert, so at a distance, the approaching car was heard as soon as it was within reasonable range; at first it started as just a suspicion, which he wanted to ignore, but he was a person that found it hard to ignore his instincts. He walked to the end of the building, to the front window, and saw the light. He pondered on what the source could be, but the only thing he could surmise was a car, and a strange one due to the suspicious way it crept, without a cause, slowly towards their front door. He was also aware that Jimmy had not returned back to the home and was expecting a call from him for a while now. It was unlike Jimmy to be so impartial to giving notice when he was going to be late, knowing he was going to be missed, given the current situation with their enemies. Nonetheless, Kane's instincts didn't like what the perception of the night was predicting itself to be. He went upstairs and got Benjamin.

They both decided to mastermind the potentially opposing situation with as much thought as possible, for it may have seemed like nothing to the naked eye, but they knew given their current situation they had to be meticulous with their decisions to dismiss what their instincts were picking up on, for it may result in the end of their lives and the lives of their family.

"The car has stop moving for about 5 minutes now", Kane stated to Benjamin, in a reasoning voice, he knew there was a somewhat sinister force at work.

There was somewhat of an irony in the situation, for the road was too dark to make out the exact shape and make of the car, otherwise they both would have known it was the car owned by Jimmy that had pulled up outside in proximity of the house. Benjamin and Kane had already pulled their weapons from hiding in anticipation of things displaying indications of danger on the uprise. Suddenly, somebody came walking on the front lawn, a somewhat unstable appearing individual, for he could hardly stand upright, and even less able to walk. It took Kane a second, then he smiled, realising it was Jimmy. Kane was about to call out to him, but Benjamin stopped him. Kane paused, and his smile then turned into varying levels of discomfort. It was puzzling, and he could not pinpoint what was on the development, but he was sure whatever the situation was it meant bad things for everyone in the house. He gripped his gun tighter.

Bullets roared from afar, directed at Jimmy, he cried out as the bullets started to hit him and shred through his body. He died within seconds, soon his body was left lifeless on the front lawn, his body started by oozing blood, but by the time he hit the ground it was merely a slow flow, as it ran across the hard dirt, it became soft and porous as the blood rushed from his body. The moment was something tragic for Benjamin, he watched in the distance behind the barriers of the home defences, his heart went out to Jimmy, overwhelmed by remorse knowing he did not have the power to save him from his ultimate demise. Even Kane watched in the distance, he did not have as long a relationship with Jimmy, but he felt somewhat similar to Benjamin. Suddenly, Benjamin's mode changed, the remorse almost like recycled fuel, for it was almost as if his blood began to boil. He became blood-thirsty, conveniently he remembered he had the AK beside him, laying on the floor. Kane always stayed with a shot and a pistol, currently his pistol laid bare in his hand, awaiting the time he had no choice but to use his weapon. Benjamin's anger was infectious, he and Kane looked at each other, almost in an admittance in a sense, reading between the lines that they may end up not making it through the situation. They were as prepared as they were ever going to be, and the fight was already initiated, thus the moment was ripe. The shooting began on both sides, starting with Benjamin and Kane through the window. For the majority of the men that Marlon and James had brought with them, they were at the forefront like pawns, for the armour-piercing bullets took the cars at the front apart, they were all injured or dead.

All that was left was Marlon and James. At this point James was already at the back of the house, he got lucky for he had come upon Amani and apprehended her, and so he came creeping through the back of the house with Amani in hand, with a pistol aimed at her head. Slowly they came wandering through the back of the house, finally Benjamin and Kane were aware as James Dillon spoke in a stern voice; "put your fucking guns down or I'll kill the bitch!"

Kane and Benjamin were caught up, they were fighting their instincts on whether to attempt to rescue Amani or to not risk her life, most likely causing her death. Kane and Benjamin decided to surrender, they dropped their weapons. James suddenly threw Amani across the room with one hand, she quickly went flying, landing just in front of Kane and Benjamin, they both took that action personally, instantly they resembled a pack of wolves, or Rottweilers on a leash waiting to shred James Dillon apart. At the front of the house, Marlon stood tall knowing that Kane and Benjamin had been disarmed. It was as if his birthday and Christmas came all in one, and he couldn't wait to reap the benefits of the gift that had been put forward for him. He waited on James, the confidence he had in James to get the job done had been immense, he had never been let down before by him. All of a sudden there was a shooting in the house, Marlon was unaware of the situation and what had taken place, but he knew it didn't make sense, James knew he wanted to personally take care of Benjamin and his family, but he stayed waiting.

5 minutes ago…

Elle-Ameen remained upstairs, all the stress and sounds of gunfire she had been hearing had her stressed, so much so that the wounds had started hurting, some of her stitches even bled, she was losing her nerve and her body was showing the symptoms accordingly. Consequently, she was on her third painkiller, trying to calm the pain and distress she was feeling, for she was panicking and unaware of what she was supposed to do, especially being in a situation she had never had to face before. Gun in hand, given to her by Benjamin, and instructions to not come downstairs no matter what happens or what she heard. However, the instructions had gone through one ear and out the next in the screams coming from Amani after James Dillon had thrown her across the room. She took to the stairs despite her condition; the pain felt from her wounds and the stress brought on by the overwhelming situation she was in. She took the stairs, gradually creeping at a gaze waiting to see what all the drama and loud sounds was about. She had come out herself to see all three of her family members standing in front of James Dillon, awaiting execution and nobody to rescue to them. At this point she had stopped thinking, it was like an out of body experience; she only came to after she had pulled the trigger and James Dillon's body had fallen to the floor, with one shot, hitting him in the back of the head. It felt like an earthquake with his body impacting the floor. In amazement, Kane, Benjamin and Amani stood still, watching in disbelief at what had just taken place. Elle-Ameen stood in shock, Benjamin walked towards her slowly, then finally unwrapped her frozen fingers from around the gun he had given her; it was as if she had put her whole body into squeezing the trigger, she stood with every muscle frozen, frantically trying to comprehend what had taken place.

Just then, there was a loud calling from the front; Marlon stood impatient calling for James to bring them out, though was patient, for at the time he felt he had the control and was in possession of the power, which he would use to eventually to take care of his enemies. Benjamin exited from the front door, with the AK pointed to Marlon's chest, while Kane came from around the back in a simultaneous fashion. As they approached Marlon who was frozen, a frantic yet nonplussed look on his face to see the two individuals he was looking at in front of him still armed, he could only surmise one thing – that James Dillon had failed. Marlon knew it was over, he did not intend to give his enemies the power to gaze at him in distress before taking his life. He smiled at Kane and Benjamin. Kane pulled the trigger, shooting him in the head. Benjamin took a deep breath, then fell to his knees, he looked over at his enemy, then walked away back to his family. Kane shared no such respect, he simply walked closer and put another bullet in his head. Just in case.

The End

GET YOUR FREE BOOK

POETRYJOURNAL DREAM.IMAGINE.EXPRESS

Dedicated to the passion of writing and the love of poetry; writing for the love of poetry and its many interpretations, and I hope that the many readers that read this book find something that they can relate to and appreciate. A fiction writing that thrives on ideals relating to the appreciation of imagination utilisation, to dream, imagine and express.
Subscribe to website:

DREAMIMAGINE.EXPRESS